Someone
Who Will Love You
in All Your
Damaged Glory

Someone
Who Will Love You
in All Your
Damaged Glory

· stories ·

RAPHAEL BOB-WAKSBERG

ALFRED A. KNOPF   NEW YORK

2019

THIS IS A BORZOI BOOK
PUBLISHED BY ALFRED A. KNOPF

Copyright © 2019 by Raphael Bob-Waksberg

www.aaknopf.com

Knopf, Borzoi Books, and the colophon are registered trademarks
of Penguin Random House LLC.

Owing to limitations on space, information on previously
published material appears on page 245.

Library of Congress Cataloging-in-Publication Data
Names: Bob-Waksberg, Raphael, [date] author.
Title: Someone who will love you in all your damaged glory :
stories / by Raphael Bob-Waksberg.
Description: First edition. | New York : Alfred A. Knopf, [2019].
Identifiers: LCCN 2018042971 (print) | LCCN 2018046016 (ebook) |
ISBN 9781524732028 (ebook) | ISBN 9781524732011 (hardcover : alk. paper)
Classification: LCC PS3602.O255 (ebook) | LCC PS3602.O255 A6 2019 (print) |
DDC 813/.6—dc23
LC record available at https://lccn.loc.gov/2018042971

Jacket images: (head) illustration by Justin Metz;
(feet) George Sheldon/Alamy; (hands) Fabrice LeRouge/Getty Images
Jacket design by Tyler Comrie

Manufactured in the United States of America
First Edition

For Dahvi,

the house where my heart lives

Contents

Contents

Someone
Who Will Love You
in All Your
Damaged Glory

The date is going well.
He's handsome, and charming,

and everything he claimed to be on the website. She likes him, she decides. He's the kind of guy you could introduce to your friends, she decides.

After dinner, he invites her back to his place. He opens a bottle of wine and pours her a glass. He also offers her a tall, skinny can with a rubber lid: "Salted circus cashew?"

"What's a circus cashew?" she asks.

"Open it up," he says. "See for yourself."

She looks at the can. The label says, The Cashew Company's Very Own, and then in big, bold letters, SALTED CIRCUS CASHEWS, and then in smaller letters, TASTY! SALTY!, and then in even smaller letters, INGREDIENTS: CASHEWS, SALT, and then on the side there's a drawing of a man with a whip—a lion tamer— the whole design of the can is circus themed—and the lion tamer has a speech balloon coming out of his mouth and inside the speech balloon it says, HELLO, FRIENDS! Please enjoy these freshly salted circus cashews, courtesy of The Cashew Company. Made with the finest ingredients, combined to perfection, this can contains only the best salted circus cashews; there certainly isn't a fake snake wrapped around a spring that will jump out and startle you when you remove the top, if that's what you were thinking. No, no, perish the thought, only cashews here, I swear to God. I am being one hundred percent sincere about the cashews. Why would there be a snake in here? That's crazy talk. Look: if you open this can and a pretend snake jumps out at you, then you have my permission to never trust me again, but why would you want to miss out on the opportunity to eat delicious salted cashews just because of the slight off-chance that this is all an elaborate ruse to make you appear foolish? Okay, I see you are still not opening the can. And I understand that. Maybe you are right to be cautious. You have been lied to before, after all. Your heart is weathered and scarred, mishandled by many, eroded by time. You're no dummy, and yet repeatedly, you stumble over the cracks of your cobblestone heart, you let your naked foolish hopes get the better of you. Perhaps every can of cashews has a fake snake lurking, but you keep opening them, stupidly, because in your heart of hearts you still believe in cashews. And every time you discover the cruel fiction of the cashew can, you swear to yourself you'll trust a little less next time, you'll be a little less open, a little more hard. It's not worth it, you say. It just isn't worth it. You're smarter than all that. From now on, you're going to be smarter. Well, I'm here to tell you that this time will be different, even though I have absolutely no evidence to support that claim. Open this can and everything will be okay. The salted circus cashews are waiting. They are so savory and delicious. You will be so glad you put your faith in me. This time is different; I promise you it's different. Why would I lie to you? Why would I want to hurt you? This time there is no snake waiting. This time things are going to be wonderful.

short stories

1. There are two kinds of people, he thought: the people you don't want to touch because you're afraid you're going to break them, and the people you don't want to touch because you're afraid they'll break you.

2. It occurred to her that she loved the *idea* of being in a relationship more than she loved any person she'd actually been in a relationship with.

3. "You're not like other girls," he said to every girl.

4. She told him she loved him and cared about him, and he was so dizzy in love himself he didn't realize she was breaking up with him.

5. He didn't trust anyone who looked better in photographs than she did in real life. He was working out a system where eventually he wouldn't have to trust anybody.

6. "I never thought I could be this happy," she imagined one day saying to someone.

7. "I don't even think about you," he couldn't wait to tell her, just as soon as she called him back.

8. He had this really amazing party trick where sometimes he could go a full hour without even once being suddenly reminded of the paralyzing truth that his life was finite and unrepeatable.

9. It occurred to her that she loved the *idea* of her husband and children and all her friends and her job and her life. She loved the idea of everything.

10. There are two kinds of people, he thought: the people you don't want to touch because you're afraid you're going to break them, and the people you want to break.

A
Most BLESSED
and AUSPICIOUS
OCCASION

So if you ever want to hear a whole bunch of people's opinions about the Right Way to Have a Wedding, the best thing to do is tell people you're getting married, and then I guarantee you will be up to your armpits in other people's opinions. For me, personally, the hearing everyone's opinion part was not the number one reason I asked Dorothy to marry me—I asked her to marry me because I love her—but as soon as we tell people, everyone takes this as their personal hand-delivered invitation to tell us exactly what we must do.

"You *must* line the aisle with candles," says Dorothy's best friend Nikki, like as soon as we tell her, like before she even says congratulations. "And the candles should ascend in height, all the way up the aisle, as a symbol for how your love and commitment grow stronger and burn brighter every day."

"We're trying to keep things small and simple," I say. "We really don't want our wedding to turn into a big, complicated production."

"But, Peter, you have to have candles," Nikki says. "Otherwise, how will the half-blind love-demon transcribe your names in the Book of Eternal Devotion?"

"Ooh." Dorothy cringes. "I forgot about the transcription of names in the Book of Eternal Devotion by the half-blind love-demon."

I squirm. "You don't think that's a little old-fashioned? I mean, my cousin Jeremy didn't have candles at his wedding, and his marriage turned out fine, even without the love-demon's transcription of names."

Dorothy darts her eyes at me and I know what she's thinking. Wasn't my cousin Jeremy just last week complaining about the new carpets his wife bought for the second Flailing Sanctuary they installed in their aboveground Prayer Hut? Maybe they'd have better communication skills if they'd had candles at their wedding so the half-blind love-demon could accurately transcribe their names in his book. I can tell this is a battle I'm not going to win, but I stress again, "Obviously, we can't do everything. We're trying to keep things simple."

Nikki is unmoved by this argument. "Okay, but how complicated is it to get candles? I'm not saying you should rent a blimp or something. It's candles. You can literally get them at the Rite Aid."

Dorothy looks at me with her big hazelnut-chocolate eyes and I know this is something she wants—even though she's the one who said in the first place that we should keep things simple.

"Well, let's just see what they have at the Rite Aid," I offer.

Dorothy lights up like the Yuletide Hogfire and I resign myself to the idea that we are definitely going to have candles of ascending height lining the aisle at our wedding.

But the main thing everyone has an opinion about is when in the ceremony to sacrifice the goats to the Stone God.

"You want to do it early," says my mother. "That way you get it out of the way and everyone knows the Stone God has been appeased, so this is a legal and blessed marriage."

"Are you kidding?" says my little brother. He's studying to be a goat slaughterer at the university, so of course he has a lot of ideas about everything. "You know how much blood that is? You have to do the slaughtering at the end, otherwise you're going to slip in goat guts while you're doing the Dance of the Cuckolded Woodland Sprite and the blood will get all over your marriage cloak and the video will end up on one of those wedding fail blogs."

In that moment, I don't have the heart to tell him we're not even planning on doing the Dance of the Cuckolded Woodland Sprite, and we probably aren't going to be wearing traditional marriage cloaks, and we *definitely* aren't hiring a videographer.

My mother shakes her head. "It's actually not that much blood"—she looks right at my brother—"if you get a good slaughterer."

His face gets all flush like it always does when he feels like no one's taking him seriously. "Even if you get the best slaughterer in town," he says, "even if you get Joseph the Forever Sanctified—"

"Please," my mother scoffs. "You couldn't *get* Joseph the Forever Sanctified with this little notice."

"Even if you could," my brother says, "I'm telling you it's going to be a lot of blood."

Dorothy puts a napkin over her pasta marinara: "I'm done eating."

"I'm sorry," I say on the drive home from the Olive Garden. "I know my family's a little intense."

"I love your family," says Dorothy. "They're just trying to help."

"We should've eloped," I say. "We could have avoided all this stress and spent the money on a honeymoon." Even as I'm saying it I know that's a stupid thing to say, because a) what money? The only reason we can afford to have a wedding at all is because Dorothy's dad is a real mover and/or shaker over at the Divinatory Rune Company and he got his branch to sponsor us. I was a little ambivalent at first about having a corporate-sponsored wedding, but it is Dorothy's dad, after all—it's not like we're just shilling for LensCrafters or something—and if it means we get to have our wedding at the Good Church, with the stained-glass windows and the comfortable seats, instead of the multipurpose room at the rec center, which, no matter how many candles you light, always smells a little like disinfectant and cottage cheese—like as if someone tried to use disinfectant to cancel out the cottage cheese smell, but then it smelled *too* much like disinfectant, so they brought in more cottage cheese, and they're still to this day struggling to get the perfect disinfectant-to-cottage-cheese ratio—well, if we can avoid that whole mess, then maybe it's worth a few tasteful Divinatory Rune Company banners and a brief mention in our vows of the many benefits and useful applications of affordable twice-sanctified divinatory runes. But, furthermore, b) even if we could afford to go somewhere for a honeymoon, we both know I couldn't take the time off. I'm already planning on working over Harvest Week, since the quarry pays time and a half on all holidays, and I'm counting on that bump to help cover rent while Dorothy's getting her master's in social work.

"Really the only thing stressing me out is the goats thing," says Dorothy. "Once we figure out what to do with the goats, everything else falls into place."

All of a sudden, I have a crazy idea. So crazy I feel like I can't even say it out loud, but as soon as it worms its way into my head I feel like I can't not say it, so I blurt out, "You want to just not sacrifice any goats?"

Dorothy is silent for a moment, and I know that as soon as I stop the car, she's going to get out and run away and never talk to me again, and the next time I see her is going to be in a photo on the cover of a trashy tabloid at the checkout line with the headline "My Fiancé Didn't Want to Sacrifice Goats!"

But instead Dorothy says, "Can we do that?"

And I say, "Dorothy, it's *our* wedding. We can do whatever we want."

She smiles, and I feel like how Clark Kent must feel when he overhears someone talking about Superman.

But doing whatever we want turns out to be a real headache when we're applying for our marriage license.

"How many goats are you going to sacrifice to the Stone God?" asks the Woman at Window Five.

"We're not going to sacrifice any goats to the Stone God," I say proudly. "It's not that kind of wedding."

The Woman looks down at her form and then back up at us. "So, just like five then?"

"No," says Dorothy. "Zero."

The man behind us in line groans and makes a big show out of looking at his watch.

"I don't understand," says the Woman. "You mean like one or two? The Stone God is not going to like getting so few goats."

"No," I say. "Not one or two. Zero. We are sacrificing zero goats to the Stone God."

She crinkles up her nose. "Well, there's not an option on the form for zero, so I'm just going to put you down for five."

Next thing I know, we get a visit from Dorothy's best friend Nikki. "I heard you're only going to sacrifice five goats."

"No—" I start to say, but she cuts me off.

"If you don't sacrifice at least thirty-eight goats, my mom's not going to come. You know she's a traditionalist about this sort of thing."

"Well, this wedding is not about your mom," snaps Dorothy. "We don't want to do the goats thing, and if she can't support that—if she can't support *us*—then your mom *shouldn't* come."

"Wow," says Nikki, and then she says again, for emphasis: *"Wow."*

Of course, my little brother is heartbroken. "What am I supposed to tell all my friends in goat-slaughtering class when it gets out that *my brother* isn't sacrificing goats at his wedding? I'll be a laughingstock!"

"It's not about you," I say. "None of this is about anybody except for the two people who are getting married to each other."

"You seem tense," says my mother. "You sure you wouldn't feel better if you just sacrificed ten goats?"

"Ten?!" says my brother. "That's an insult! Honestly, at that point you're better off just not sacrificing any and hoping the Stone God doesn't notice."

"Yeah," I say. "That's the idea."

"Okay," says my mother, "forget about the goats. But I'm worried about you and Dorothy, trying to organize this whole thing by yourselves."

"It's not a 'whole thing,'" I say. "That's actually kind of the point, that it's not a 'whole thing.'"

"Why don't you meet with a wedding planner? Maybe having someone else will ease the tension off the two of you."

"There's no tension," I say, a little too loud and a little too fast, in a manner that makes it seem like there is definitely some tension.

"It sounds like there's some tension," observes my little brother, who when he's done learning about slaughtering goats could probably benefit from a class in minding his own business.

"The only tension is coming from the outside," I say. "It's outside tension. There's no tension between Dorothy and me. Besides, who's going to pay for a wedding planner? I can't ask Dorothy's dad for more money."

"So, don't hire a wedding planner," says my mom. "Just meet with one, see what she has to say."

So we set up a meeting with Clarissa the Planner of Weddings.

"The first thing you need to know about us," Dorothy says to Clarissa the Planner of Weddings, "is that we're really not looking for a big, complicated extravaganza with a lot of moving parts," and I'm so happy that Dorothy says this, confirming again that we are in fact one hundred percent not having tension.

"Okay," says Clarissa. "What *are* you looking for?"

"It's very simple," I say. "We walk down the aisle. Dorothy looks beautiful. I'm wearing a suit. The officiant says a few words about love. Then I say a few words. Then Dorothy says a few words. Maybe Aunt Estelle reads a Gertrude Stein poem. Then the officiant says, 'Well, do you love each other?' I say, 'Yep.' Dorothy says, 'Yep.' Then we kiss and everyone claps, and then we dance—"

"The Dance of the Cuckolded Woodland Sprite?"

"No. Not the Dance of the Cuckolded Woodland Sprite. Just normal dancing. Like 'Twist and Shout' or 'Crazy in Love.' That kind of thing. We do that for a couple hours, and then everyone goes home. Just like your basic Ikea one-size-fits-all wedding."

"But that's so unromantic," says Dorothy's best friend Nikki, who is also at this meeting for some reason.

"It's actually very romantic," I say, "because it's just about us. It's not about all this other stuff that has nothing to do with us."

"What does Gertrude Stein have to do with anything?" scoffs Nikki.

Dorothy smiles. "We both love Gertrude Stein. On one of our first dates we went to see *Doctor Faustus Lights the Lights*."

"I love that part," says the Planner of Weddings. "It's special, it's specific to you, and it means something. But I do want to circle back to the whole not-having-a-big-ceremony thing. How solid are you on that idea, one to ten?"

"Ten," I say.

"Ten," says Dorothy.

"Okay, so pretty solid, but maybe there's a little bit of wiggle room there?"

"No," I say.

"No," says Dorothy.

"Okay, I love that you two are on the same page. I do want to make sure you're thinking about all this practically, though, because part of the reason for having a big ceremony is that it could get interrupted at any time by the sudden Weeping and Flailing and Shouting of Lamentations by the Shrieking Chorus. The Weeping and Flailing and Shouting of Lamentations could go on for at least twenty minutes—so if you don't have enough other stuff going on, suddenly the whole thing becomes *about* the Shrieking Chorus, and then you're not getting that special small feeling you're looking for. Trust me, I've seen it happen."

Dorothy sinks in her chair, and I try to stay strong, for both of us.

"But that's part of what I'm saying. We're not going to have a Shrieking Chorus."

Dorothy spins like a lighthouse and shines directly at me, "Wait, are we really not having a Shrieking Chorus?"

"That's half the fun of a wedding!" says Nikki.

"It is not half the fun," I protest, but Nikki doubles down:

"Literally fifty percent of the fun of a wedding is that you never know when the Shrieking Chorus is going to start the Weeping and Flailing and Shouting of Lamentations. If you don't have a Shrieking Chorus, why are you even having a wedding?"

"Because we love each other," I argue meekly, and I feel like if I have to say it one more time, we won't even need a Shrieking Chorus, because I will start Weeping and Flailing and Shouting Lamentations all by myself.

Dorothy's still mulling it over. "I guess it never occurred to me that we wouldn't even have a *small* Shrieking Chorus. It doesn't really feel like a wedding without one."

The Planner of Weddings grimaces, like she's really embarrassed that we're having this discussion in front of her, like this is the first time she's ever seen a couple have a disagreement about the details of a wedding. "It sounds like you two need to have some more conversations with each other before I can really know how to help you."

"Definitely," says Nikki proudly, and I think that if Nikki loves Clarissa so much, maybe they should be the ones getting married, and then they can have all the Shrieking Choruses they want.

At this point, we could both use a pick-me-up, so I take Dorothy to the ceremonial egg store to look at the Promise Eggs. I know technically it's bad luck for a bride to see her Promise Egg before the ceremony, but it is becoming increasingly apparent that Dorothy has maybe more Ideas About This Wedding than she initially let on when we Decided Together that we were Both Cool with a Very Easy, Very Small Wedding Without Frills or Complications, and it is furthermore becoming increasingly apparent that if I go pick out a Promise Egg without her input I'm going to screw it up, and then it's going to sit in a display case in our living room for the rest of our marriage—a testament to how badly I screwed it up, a testament to how I always screw things up, a testament to how I will continue to screw things up forever.

Everyone at the ceremonial egg store is very friendly and excited for us. "Congratulations!" says Sabrina the Person of Sales. "You guys are an amazing couple, I can already tell, and I want to help you find the *perfect* Promise Egg. Tell me what you're looking for. Just shout some words at me, let's get real loose."

"Something on the smaller side," I say, "maybe one and a half to two feet tall?"

Sabrina nods. "Small eggs are very in right now; you have excellent taste. Are we thinking silver? Platinum? Rose gold?"

I somehow muster the confidence to mumble, "We were thinking maybe we could start with the copper ones?"

Sabrina doesn't miss a beat: "Of course! We have some lovely copper eggs, that's a fabulous place to start. I'm going to go pull some options."

"Sorry," Dorothy says, "I know you probably get paid on commission."

Sabrina laughs. "We're going to find something amazing, I promise." She squeezes Dorothy's arm and heads to the back room.

"You don't need to apologize," I say.

"I feel bad."

"We belong here just as much as anybody," I tell Dorothy and also myself.

Sabrina the Person of Sales shows us a series of copper eggs, each just slightly more expensive than I was hoping to pay, each just slightly not quite the Promise Egg that Dorothy always imagined for herself. She puts on a brave face, but I can hear the disappointment in her voice when she says, "This one kind of feels like the Promise Egg my grandparents have."

Sabrina nods. "Well, the copper eggs do tend to be a little more . . . traditional."

Across the shop, another couple is having a blast in the platinum egg section. The man is trying to lift a four-foot egg and making a lot of goofy faces. They look like they got dressed up special just for going shopping, or else maybe right after getting the egg, they're going yachting or golfing or something, or else maybe they just always dress this nice. I suddenly notice how dirty my jeans are.

"You don't have anything maybe a little nicer than these?" I ask. I've been in houses with copper Promise Eggs before, and they've always seemed adequate, but here in the store, next to all the other eggs, it's clear how dinky and unremarkable they are. I watch Dorothy run her finger over the crude butterfly molding on one of the eggs, and I can tell she's thinking the same thing, even though she would never admit it.

"Do you want to maybe look at some silver ones?" asks Sabrina. "I get that you don't want anything too fancy, but we have some very modest options in silver."

Dorothy looks at me, like, *Can we?*

"Let's just *look* at the silver eggs," I say, a sentence that immediately vaults to the top of the Dumbest Things I've Ever Said chart, barely edging out "Can I get it extra spicy?" and "I liked the way your hair looked before."

Sabrina the Person of Sales takes us into a back room, and the first thing she shows us is a 1954 Felix Wojnowski silver egg, adorned with rare gems and festooned with religious iconography.

"This one's probably a little too showy, don't you think?" I say, assuring everyone in the room that my primary concern lies not in matters of price but in ostentation.

"I don't know," says Dorothy, "I think it's nice."

"Yeah," I say, "it's definitely nice, but maybe a little too showy?"

"How about this one?" asks Sabrina. "This is the new trend—it's silver plated, so it's elegant but it doesn't feel too heavy."

Dorothy nods. "You hear that, Peter? Silver *plated*."

I smile and glance down at the price tag—it's eight times what the most expensive copper eggs cost.

"Yeah, these are some great options," I say. "You're really giving us a lot to think about."

But Dorothy is done thinking. "I want to be surprised at the wedding so I'm going to go wait in the car. Peter, I'm sure I'm going to love whatever you pick."

She heads out, and Sabrina smiles at me and says, "Should we look at some platinum options?"

I cringe. "I wish you could see our apartment. People like us don't normally get Promise Eggs like these."

"Well, it actually isn't uncommon for a Promise Egg to be the nicest thing you own," Sabrina offers helpfully.

"Do you think if I get a copper one, Dorothy will hate me forever?"

"Of course not! She said she'll love whatever you pick, and I think it's important to take people at their word."

I nod.

"That said," she continues for some reason, "her eyes really lit up when she saw the Wojnowski."

I think about Dorothy. I think about our first date, when I tried to take her to the drive-in movie, but my credit card was declined. I felt like a real idiot, but she had the idea to drive up the hill and watch the whole thing without sound. We made up the dialogue ourselves, which turned out to be even more fun and romantic in a stupid sort of way, and I promised myself that night that I would do whatever I could to love this woman for the rest of my life.

"Can you just hold on to the Wojnowski?" I ask. "I can't afford it—*now*—but I want to get it."

Sabrina grimaces. "I'm really not supposed to . . . but you guys seem so in love . . . I could probably stash it somewhere for a couple weeks." She winks at me, and my heart is full of baby birds leaping into flight, and I make a mental note to write a good review on Yelp and also to name our first daughter after Sabrina the Person of Sales.

I slide into the car and Dorothy says, "Don't tell me what you got. I want to be surprised."

"I didn't get anything," I say. "I decided to make an egg myself out of construction paper and pipe cleaners."

"Har-har." Then: "Not really, though, right?"

"I thought you wanted to be surprised."

"This must be a great place to work," says Dorothy, "because all day you're around happy couples who are in love and you're helping them plan their future together."

I say, "Yeah, and you don't even need a master's in social work."

Dorothy gives me a look like, *Okay, buddy.*

And I give her a look like, *I'm just saying!*

And she gives me a look like, *What am I going to do with you?*

The good news is the very next day there's an accident at the quarry and Frankie Scharff breaks her fibula. This is not good news for Frankie Scharff, who already has a husband on disability, or for Joey Zlotnik, the guy who has to climb the ladder to reset the DAYS SINCE A WORK-RELATED ACCIDENT sign, because while he's trying to maneuver around the giant zero, he falls off the ladder and breaks his fibula—but it's great news for me, because it means I can pick up extra shifts at the quarry. That itself is a mixed blessing, I know, because the more hours I work the more likely it is that I'll have an accident and break my fibula, but as I see it, the pros outweigh the cons. As I see it, the pros are:

1. It makes me look like a real go-getter and team player to David and David in the front office.

2. I get paid more money. This is a crucial pro, because it means I can cover unplanned-for expenses as they arise, such as, say, when my fiancée suddenly decides she wants a Wojnowski Promise Egg or a Shrieking Chorus at our wedding, even though she knows that those are things we did not budget for.

3. I get paid more money. This is related to the previous pro, but not exactly the same. The previous "I get paid more money" is a practical matter, but this one is more spiritual. While I'm working extra hours at the quarry, I can think about how I'm earning more money to cover the wedding and also cover the life I'm going to spend with my future wife. This gives me a good feeling, to be a provider, which is so embarrassing and old-fashioned, and if anyone asked me about it I'd deny it, but the truth is it feels good.

4. It keeps me away from fighting with Dorothy about wedding stuff. This one I feel less good about, but the truth is the closer we get to the wedding, the more we argue. Our newest disagreement is about whether to take part in the traditional Week of Lying with the Grand Priest Kenny Sorgenfrei.

"I have to lie with the Grand Priest Kenny Sorgenfrei," Dorothy says, "so he can confirm to the whole village I am a virgin."

"But you're not a virgin," I say. "Neither of us is."

"That's not the point," she says. "It's tradition. If the Grand Priest Kenny Sorgenfrei doesn't tell the whole village I'm a virgin my mother will be mortified."

So she goes to lie with the grand priest, and I work more hours at the quarry.

I bring a casserole to Frankie Scharff's place. This is maybe a mistake, because even though Frankie's real glad to see a friend from work, the whole situation really bums me out. She's in a tiny apartment with her husband and three kids. I feel bad for judging, because of course we're all doing what we can, but the sink is full of dishes, the walls are water damaged—again, it's not Frankie's fault, or the fault of her husband, who really is a decent guy—but the worst part of all is the Promise Egg on display in the corner. I recognize it as one of the copper eggs from the store—one I had half convinced myself to buy for Dorothy and me. In the shop, it looked simple, modest—elegant even—but in Frankie's apartment I see it for what it really is: cheap.

I go back to the egg store and I buy the Wojnowski. I put it on two credit cards. I figure if I take all my vacation days on non-holidays, I can work over the holidays and get overtime for it.

Do I want to pay fifty dollars more to get our names engraved on the 1954 Felix Wojnowski sterling silver egg? You bet I do. Do I also want to buy the special display case that goes with the egg? Absolutely. And who's going to hold the egg during the ceremony?

"We can rent a eunuch for you through the Church of the Wine God," offers Sabrina the Person of Sales. "They know what they're doing. The Wojnowski is heavier than it looks, and I've seen more than one wedding ruined because they asked a random uncle to hold the Promise Egg and then he dropped it in the middle of the ceremony."

"Okay," I say. "Let's get that eunuch!"

That night I'm too excited to sleep, so I drive to the ravine and look out over the water. I think about Dorothy, currently lying with the grand priest, with no idea what her future husband just did for her. I know the egg doesn't matter; I know what really matters is how much I love her—but the egg is a symbol for that love, and when I think about what a nice symbol I got I feel proud and I feel lucky and I feel blessed. I think about Dorothy—I think about the way she rests her head on my chest as we fall asleep—and I feel proud and I feel lucky and I feel blessed.

Then the worst possible thing happens: Gavin Cachefski works a double shift at the quarry and conks out at the power drill and five guys end up breaking their fibulas.

David and David call an all-staff meeting.

"No more double shifts," says one of the Davids, the David who talks. "Too many guys are breaking their fibulas."

The crowd groans and the other David, the one who doesn't talk, whispers something in the first David's ear.

"Also," says David, "as of today, we are no longer offering time and a half for work over holidays."

"That's not fair!" I shout. "I've been counting on that money."

"Me too!" shouts Jose, whose kitchen recently fell into a sinkhole.

"We all have!" shouts Deb, who has a kid with real silly bones.

"It's not about the money," says David. "This is about your safety. We're a family here at the quarry, and if we keep breaking fibulas on the job, our insurance rates go way up and then we're going to have to start laying people off. We really don't want to do that because, again: family."

"So you're saying we can't work over the holidays?"

The David who doesn't talk whispers something into the ear of the David who does talk and he nods. "No, you definitely can," he says. "In fact, we'd appreciate it if you would; we just can't pay you time and a half, because that would be incentivizing it."

"Unbelievable!" says Kath Chung.

Kath is a real rabble-rouser, and for a moment it seems like she's really about to start rousing some rabble, but before she can get too into it, the David who doesn't talk says loudly, "This is not up for debate," and we all at once realize the severity of the moment, because when the David who doesn't talk talks, that's when you know things have gotten serious.

I return to the egg store. Sabrina the Person of Sales greets me with a big smile. "Hey, big guy! Did you want to take another gander at your masterpiece?"

I can't look her in the eye. "I need to trade it in. It's too much."

She looks at me like I'm speaking another language. "You can't trade it in. You already got it engraved."

"Okay, well, can I at least get the money back for the eunuch? We don't need him. We'll just leave the egg in the stand."

"That was a donation to the Church of the Wine God. You can't just take that back."

"Sabrina, you gotta help me out here. Is there *anything* you can do for me?"

Sabrina looks both ways, then leans in and whispers, "I can give you a coupon for twenty percent off your next purchase."

I explode: "Why would I ever need to purchase *another* Promise Egg?!"

Not knowing what else to do, I hightail it to the Divinatory Rune Company and take the elevator all the way to the top. Dorothy's father is in his office, looking out his window over the factory floor, overseeing the polishing and blessing of Divinatory Runes.

"Peter! What can I do you for?"

"Well . . . it's about the wedding."

"Oh?"

"It's about money."

"Oh."

And I mumble mumble something Promise Egg mumble mumble can't afford it.

Dorothy's father sits down. He looks pained. "The Promise Egg symbolizes the promise you're making to my daughter—the promise to provide for her and keep her safe. If I'm paying for it, what kind of message does that send?"

"I can work it off," I say. "After my shift at the quarry, let me come here for a stint on the polishing line. Dorothy doesn't even have to know."

He takes a deep breath and looks at me like I'm a salad he just found a dead bug in and he's trying to figure out whether it's worth it to call the waitress over and send me back.

"Peter, I really wish you'd reconsider, about the goats."

This throws me for a loop, because by this point, I honestly thought the goat thing was settled.

"As per the goats of it all—" I start to say, but I'm immediately thrown off by the weirdness of starting a sentence with the phrase "as per the goats of it all." That was a poor choice. I thought I could pull it off. I couldn't pull it off.

"Look," he says. "I get it. At our wedding, we wanted to keep things small, so we only sacrificed twelve goats. But if you don't sacrifice *any* goats, the Stone God is going to get angry and he's going to put a curse on your house and your first baby will come out a statue. Now, that's something I simply won't allow."

"Sir," I say, and it feels weird to call him sir, because when Dorothy and I first announced our engagement, he gave me a big hug and told me to call him Dad, but in this moment I know it would be even weirder to call him Dad. "Sir, with all due respect, has that ever actually happened? Has anyone actually not done the sacrifice and then given birth to a statue?"

"It happened to Kyle's Wife, in chapter twelve, verse eight of the Book of Kyle."

"Well, yeah, of course, obviously it happens in the Book of Kyle, but I mean has it ever happened to anyone you actually know, in your lifetime?"

He takes a long drag off his cigar, the whole time looking me square in the eye.

"Everyone *I* know," he says, "made a sacrifice to the Stone God."

He pulls out a pen that probably costs more than I get paid in a year and starts scribbling in a checkbook. "I'll tell you what," he says. "You want to sacrifice goats, I'll pay for the goats—I'll pay for however many goats you want, and I'll even throw in a sizable chunk on top for the slaughterer. You want to ask your brother to slaughter the goats and use the money I give you on something else, well, that's your business . . ."

"I appreciate that, but all I'm asking for is—"

"I think my offer is quite reasonable," he says.

I nod, ashamed I even tried to negotiate with the guy who basically runs the local branch of the Divinatory Rune Company.

"And I like to think I'm a reasonable man. A modern, sophisticated, sensible man. But no daughter of mine is getting married at a wedding without goat slaughter."

I go to the House of Sorgenfrei. Kenny answers the door in a bathrobe. "Hey, brother."

"I need to talk to Dorothy."

"Ooh, no can do, buddy. The groom is not supposed to see the bride as she lies with the grand priest."

"I have to talk to her. Tell her it's an emergency."

Kenny Sorgenfrei pouts, squints at me, then closes the door. A few minutes later, Dorothy emerges in a bathrobe. "What is it? What's wrong?"

"First of all, hi. You look beautiful."

"Peter, what is going on?"

"I've been thinking about the wedding and I think we should sacrifice goats."

Dorothy quickly whittles the word "furious" into a verb and furiouses at me, *"That's* the emergency?"

"Well, the wedding's in two weeks and I need to put an order in at the wholesale goat outlet . . ."

"Okay, so when I want to lie with the grand priest it's stupid and old-fashioned, but because your brother slaughters goats, suddenly—"

"No, it's not about that."

"Weren't you the one who wanted to keep things small?"

"Actually," I say, *"you* were the one who wanted to keep things small. But we can just sacrifice ten goats. What's the big deal? It'll make a lot of people happy."

She tightens her bathrobe. "If today we say we're sacrificing ten goats, tomorrow it's going to be twenty-eight, and then before we know it we're going to be one of those two-hundred-goat weddings where most of the ceremony is spent sacrificing goats."

"I'm just saying if the Stone God does put a curse on our house and our first baby comes out a statue, you're the one who's going to have to give birth to it."

She takes a deep breath, and for a second it feels like that's going to be the end of it, but then she says, "Look," and if there's one thing I know about being in a relationship, it's that no good sentence starts with the word "look." No one ever says, "Look. That's a great point! You're right! Let's stop arguing now!"

"Look," she says. "I've been doing a lot of thinking. Partly on my own, and partly . . . in conversation with the Grand Priest Kenny Sorgenfrei."

"Conversation? What conversation?"

"Multiple conversations, Peter."

"Why are you having multiple conversations with Kenny Sorgen-frei? You're just supposed to lie with him—you don't need to have conversations."

"Sometimes, after we lie with each other, we have conversations."

"That's not part of it. Since when is that part of it?"

"*Some* guys," she says, with an edge in her voice, "like to talk after, instead of just going to sleep. It's actually kind of nice."

"Okay, so you have conversations. What are these conversations about?"

"As you know, Kenny lies with a lot of brides—like, most brides—and he says he doesn't usually see brides who have so many . . . doubts."

Well, if there's one other thing I know about being in a relation-ship, it's that even worse than saying "Look" is when someone says "I have doubts."

"You have doubts?"

"Yeah, I have a few doubts."

Suddenly I feel like I'm talking to some other Dorothy—a new, different Dorothy I don't know how to talk to. I try to catch her eye, but she won't look at me. "You're having conversations, you're having doubts—what's going on with you?"

"Recently you've been spending so much time at the quarry. I feel like I never see you, and . . . I don't think that augurs well for our marriage."

"It doesn't 'augur well'? Who says 'augur well'? Did Kenny Sor-genfrei say that?"

"Well, he put it into words, but I was separately feeling already like the auguring of it wasn't so good."

"I've been busting my ass at the quarry so I could afford to give you the perfect wedding."

"It doesn't feel that way. It feels like you've been working late hours because you don't want to be around me."

"You think I don't want to be around you?"

"I'm just saying it feels that way!"

"Well, if I don't want to be around you, then why am I marrying you?"

"I don't know!" she shouts. "Why are you?!"

I immediately think of a hundred Wrong Things to Say, but I can't for the life of me think of a single Right Thing to Say, so instead I shout the most un-Wrong of the Wrong Things I can think of, which is "All the normal reasons!"

I have never heard a person say a sentence with such disdain as the way Dorothy spits back at me, *"All the normal reasons?"*

"Yeah," I say. "The normal reasons. Like, I love you and I want to spend the rest of my life with you. It's all the dumb clichés about how even when I'm mad at you I love you and how every day the best part of it is waking up next to you. And it kills me that this is all the normal, typical people-in-love stuff, because I want to believe our love is special—that it's bigger and more interesting than any love that anyone else has had before—but the heartbreaking truth is my love for you is so consistent and predictable and boring."

I can see Dorothy soften a little, which is good, because I don't have anything else to say.

"Is that why you want goats at our wedding?"

"As per the goats of it all . . . I promised your dad we would have them. I needed more money from him because I got you the Felix Wojnowski Promise Egg and I couldn't afford it."

Dorothy holds a hand up to her mouth. Her eyes go wide. "You got the Wojnowski?"

"Yeah," I say. "It's stupid. The whole thing is stupid. But . . . I love you."

Dorothy smiles. "Well, there's nothing stupid about that," she says in a detached-adjacent tone I can tell she intends to sound cool, but because her voice cracks and her eyes sparkle with tears, it comes across like the most sincere thing in the world.

"No?" I ask, and she shakes her head.

"Are you kidding?" she says, gently, sweetly. "I'm a godsdamn delight."

Now, let me tell you, I thought Dorothy was beautiful before, but when I'm standing at the altar and I see her walk into the Good Church in her marriage cloak—the stained-glass windows behind her—well, I could live to be a hundred and it would still be the loveliest thing I'd ever seen. And in that moment I think: This is the best possible way to have a wedding, because it's the kind of wedding where while it's happening, I get to marry Dorothy.

My little brother does the goat sacrifice himself—we settle on fifty goats, a good round number—and it goes off without a hitch, except for a half hour later, during Aunt Estelle's reading of the Gertrude Stein poem, it turns out one of the goats didn't all the way die and it bucks off the sacrificial altar and scrambles up and down the aisle, braying and squealing and shooting blood everywhere. My little brother jumps up and tries to tackle it, but it's a slippery little thing, all lubed up with the blood and guts of forty-nine other goats. Blood is squirting everywhere, and my mother leans in and whispers, "This is why you get a professional goat slaughterer."

Of course, this sets off one of the guys in the Shrieking Chorus.

He starts Weeping and Flailing and Shouting Lamentations. And then the guy next to him starts Weeping and Flailing and Shouting Lamentations. And before you know it all twelve of them are climbing over the pews, their eyes rolled back in their heads, Weeping and Flailing and Shouting Lamentations.

Meanwhile, Aunt Estelle is still reading the Gertrude Stein poem, and she doesn't know what to do, so she just starts reading it louder and louder.

My mother leans in and whispers, "For Gods' sake, will you go help your little brother?"

I run into the aisle, and my brother chases the goat right into my arms. I slip in blood and fall on my ass, but I hold tight of the wriggling thing so it can't escape. My brother is shaking, and I realize too late why most couples wait until the *end* of the wedding to give the ceremonial goat-slaughtering knife to the youngest cousin to throw into the ravine. It always felt so anticlimactic to end with that, which is why we sent little Tucker off early, but now I get it. You're going to want to hold on to that knife.

"What now?" my brother asks.

"I don't know!" I shout, while struggling to get a better grip on the convulsing beast. "You're supposed to be the big goat expert!"

Then Dorothy shouts something, but I can't quite hear her over the chaos and also Aunt Estelle. Dorothy shouts again and points to the eunuch at the back of the church, and I yell to my brother, "The egg!"

He runs back and wrestles the big silver thing out of the eunuch's hands. The eunuch has taken an oath to the Wine God to protect the egg at all costs until the end of the ceremony, so he doesn't let it go easily, but then my brother punches him in the face and he staggers back. I cringe, thinking about how this must look to Dorothy's side of the family—not to mention the Wine God, if He even really exists—and I'm sure my mother is thinking that she raised us boys better than that, but sometimes desperate times call for punching a eunuch in the face so you can steal his giant silver egg and use it as a blunt object.

By this point, the Shrieking Chorus has started Weeping and Flailing their way into the aisle, so my brother has no choice but to run all the way around the side of the congregation to get back to me and the goat.

I lie on my back and try to position the squirming animal in such a way that my brother can bash its head in quickly. He holds the egg high in the air, but then the goat's eye twitches and looks up at him and suddenly my little brother melts.

"Come on!" I shout, as the goat bucks in my arms and kicks me in the stomach. "What are you waiting for?"

"I can't," says my little brother. "I can't do it."

He falls to his knees and cradles the silver egg in his arms like a baby. I feel bad for him, but also I can't help but think about all the money my parents wasted sending him to the university so he could major in goat slaughtering.

"Screw it," says Dorothy's best friend Nikki. "I'll do it."

Nikki squeezes into the aisle and grabs the egg from my brother, but in her eagerness she knocks over one of the aisle-lining candles of ascending height, and when the flames hit the bottom of her dress, the whole thing lights up like a Yuletide Hogfire. Nikki drops the egg and runs up and down the aisle all aflame. She's screaming, and the goat's screaming, and then everyone else starts screaming, except for Aunt Estelle, who, Gods bless her, has a job to do and isn't going to sit down until she finishes her poem.

I look at my bride, who is standing at the altar, frozen, mouth agape—mouth very agape—like for real I guarantee you've never seen a mouth so agape.

She looks at me with her big forest-flavored eyes, like, *Can you believe this?*

And I look at her, like, *Well, what did we expect?*

The goat convulses in my arms, and Dorothy starts laughing. Then she puts her arm up and juts her chin out, like she's about to start doing the Dance of the Cuckolded Woodland Sprite, and I start laughing. She's laughing, and I'm laughing, and I swear to Gods I'm the luckiest man in the world. I look at her, lit by fire, caked in blood, scored by the Shrieking of the Chorus and the wailing of a dying goat, and I wish I could marry her again. I wish I could marry her a hundred thousand times.

Missed Connection—m4w

I saw you on the Manhattan-bound Brooklyn Q train.

I was wearing a blue-striped T-shirt and a pair of maroon pants.
You were wearing a vintage green skirt and a cream-colored top.

You got on at DeKalb and sat across from me, and we made eye
contact, briefly. I fell in love with you a little bit, in that stupid
way where you completely make up a fictional version of the
person you're looking at and fall in love with that person. But
still, I think there was something there.

Several times we looked at each other and then looked away.
I tried to think of something to say to you—maybe pretend
I didn't know where I was going and ask you for directions,
or say something nice about your boot-shaped earrings,
or just say, "Hot day." It all seemed so stupid.

At one point, I caught you staring at me and you immediately
averted your eyes. You pulled a book out of your bag and started
reading it—a biography of Lyndon Johnson—but I noticed you
never once turned a page.

My stop was Union Square, but at Union Square I decided to
stay on, rationalizing that I could just as easily transfer to the 7

at 42nd Street, but then I didn't get off at 42nd Street either. You must have missed your stop as well, because when we got all the way to the end of the line at 96th, we both just sat there in the car, waiting.

I looked over at you and tilted my head, curious. You shrugged and held up your book; you'd missed your stop because you were distracted, that's all.

We took the train all the way back down—down the Upper East Side, weaving through midtown, from Times Square to Herald Square to Union Square, under SoHo and Chinatown, up across the bridge back into Brooklyn, past Barclays and Prospect Park, past Flatbush and Midwood and Sheepshead Bay, all the way to Coney Island. And when we got to Coney Island, I knew I had to say something.

Still I said nothing.

And so we went back up.

Up and down the Q line, over and over. We caught the rush-hour crowds and then saw them thin out again. We watched the sun set over Manhattan as we crossed the East River. I gave myself deadlines: I'll talk to her before Newkirk; I'll talk to her before Canal. Still, I remained silent.

For months we sat on the train saying nothing. We survived on bags of Skittles sold to us by kids raising money for their basketball teams. We must have heard a million mariachi bands, had our faces nearly kicked in by a hundred thousand break-dancers. I gave money to the panhandlers until I ran out of singles. When the train went aboveground I'd get text messages and voice mails ("Where are you? What happened? Are you okay?") until my phone battery ran out.

I'll talk to her before daybreak; I'll talk to her before Tuesday. The longer I waited, the harder it got. What could I possibly say to you now, now that we'd passed this same station for the hundredth time? Maybe if I could go back to the first time the Q switched over to the local R line for the weekend, I could have said, "Well, this is inconvenient," but I couldn't say it now, could I? I would kick myself for days after every time you sneezed— why hadn't I said "Bless you"? That tiny gesture could have been enough to pivot us into a conversation, but here in stupid silence we sat.

There were nights when we were the only two souls in the car, perhaps even on the whole train, and even then I felt self-conscious about bothering you. She's reading her book, I thought, she doesn't want to talk to me. Still, there were moments when I felt a connection. Someone would shout something crazy about Jesus and we'd immediately look at each other to register our reactions. A couple of teenagers would exit, holding hands, and we'd both think: Young love.

For sixty years, we sat in that car, just barely pretending not to notice each other. I got to know you so well, if only peripherally. I memorized the folds of your body, the contours of your face, the patterns of your breath. I saw you cry once after you'd glanced at a neighbor's newspaper. I wondered if you were crying about something specific or just the general passage of time, so unnoticeable until suddenly noticeable. I wanted to comfort you, wrap my arms around you, assure you everything would be fine, but it felt too familiar; I stayed glued to my seat.

One day, in the middle of the afternoon, you stood up as the train pulled into Avenue J. It was difficult for you, this simple task of standing up—you hadn't done it in sixty years. Holding on to the rails, you managed to get yourself to the door. You hesitated briefly there, perhaps waiting for me to say something, giving me one last chance to stop you, but rather than spit out a lifetime of suppressed almost-conversations, I said nothing, and I watched you slip out between the closing sliding doors.

It took a few more stops before I realized you were really gone. I kept waiting for you to reenter the subway car, sit down next to me, rest your head on my shoulder. Nothing would be said. Nothing would need to be said.

When the train returned to Avenue J, I craned my neck as we entered the station. Perhaps you were there, on the platform, still waiting. Perhaps I would see you, smiling and bright, your long white hair waving in the wind from the oncoming train.

But no, you were gone. And I realized most likely I would never see you again. And I thought about how amazing it is that you can know somebody for sixty years and yet still not really know that person at all.

I stayed on the train until it got to Union Square, at which point I got off and transferred to the L.

The
Serial Monogamist's Guide
to Important New York City Landmarks

Towering over the east side of Fifth Avenue, between Fiftieth and Fifty-First Streets, you'll find the majestic St. Patrick's Cathedral, historically significant as the place where you and Eric sat on the steps and ate frozen yogurt that time.

Should you happen upon this neo-Gothic-style still-active Roman Catholic church, you'll be instantly transported to that ancient day, several summers prior, when the two of you were finally getting along again, for the first time in what seemed like forever. It felt like old times, this excursion into Manhattan, and you smiled as the sticky-sweet swirl of hazelnut and banana melted down your arm.

At one point, Eric looked at you and, grinning, said, "Hey, you've got a little . . ." and as he reached for your face, you instinctively jerked away from his hand. You didn't mean anything by it, this flinch—it just happened—but in an instant, the whole day fell apart.

You and Eric looked at each other, in the shadow of that cathedral, and you saw Eric's face fall, as you had often seen it fall, in that just-so-Eric way.

"What are we doing?" Eric asked, and you shook your head and said, "I don't know."

And then the two of you sat on the steps of the cathedral for a very long time without saying anything.

Later, you and Eric went back to his apartment and had sex. But it was too late. The damage had been done.

New York City is full of history. Take, for example, the Waverly Diner down in Greenwich Village. It was at this very spot you and Keith stayed up all night talking over pancakes, after ducking out of Emily's twenty-sixth birthday party.

There was so much to say to each other, you and Keith. It was right after you and Eric broke up, and Keith was so not Eric. Keith was like the opposite of everything Eric stood for.

If you had been thinking rationally at the time, you probably could've guessed that you would end up hurting Keith in ways he didn't deserve. But that night everything seemed so perfect. You wanted Keith, and you felt like you had earned him somehow. It felt like all your life had been persistently preparing you for meeting this man.

You still sometimes pass the Waverly Diner, down in Greenwich Village, on the Avenue of the Americas, but you rarely go inside it, and you never order the pancakes.

Was ever a city so ruined by history, so smothered in the blood of past conflagration? Once, while haphazardly browsing the Restoration Hardware on Ninth Avenue and Thirteenth, killing time before meeting Boris's parents for a walk up the High Line, you idly picked up a loose spatula that suddenly reminded you of a fight you'd had two years earlier in Keith's kitchen.

The conversation had started innocuously enough when Keith asked, "What do you want in your omelet?" and somehow ended two hours later when he shouted, "I don't think you really love me; I think you're just terrified of being alone," and you, gesticulating wildly with the spatula, spat back without thinking, "I *am* alone; you have no idea how alone I am," as if that were some kind of comeback.

The spatula you now held in the Restoration Hardware was the same, the architecture of it surprisingly familiar, the weight of it in your hand alarmingly potent, and when you breathlessly explained to Boris the story of the artifact's eerie significance, he scrunched up his nose and said, "If the two of us are ever going to move forward, at some point, you're going to have to stop looking backward."

You'd already started dating Sean when Boris called, late, drunk, and asked if you wanted to go to Staten Island. You'd never been to Staten Island, and Boris had never been to Staten Island, and since Boris was about to move to Philadelphia, this seemed like as good a time as any to visit Staten Island.

Boris had also invited you to go to Philadelphia with him, but that felt too far, too much, too soon, too Boris. Instead, you chose New York. You broke up with Boris, got your own place in Bushwick, and started dating Sean, the cute bartender at Union Pool. You didn't think you'd see Boris again, but on his last night in New York he called you, late, drunk, to invite you on an adventure.

The truth is there's not much to see on Staten Island, not after midnight anyway. The boat ride there is awfully romantic, but once you get there . . . well, there's the elevator ride up to the top floor of the ferry building, and if you're bored, you can take it back down again.

There's a fish tank in the ferry building and some reading material posted at the base of it about the logistics of housing a fish tank in the Staten Island ferry building. It's a very large fish tank, so heavy the floor has to be supported with iron beams. "It's a big deal, this fish tank; a lot of work went into it," says the placard at the base, to the best of your recollection (you haven't been back). "We did this all for you, visitors to Staten Island, so you'd better appreciate it!"

You remember standing next to Boris and reading the fish tank placard. You would have thought there'd be more to say to each other this night before you said good-bye forever, but it turns out you'd already said everything. So instead of going through it all again, you stood side by side in the silence of the ferry building and read the information at the base of the fish tank.

"Welcome to Staten Island," it probably said. "We hope you enjoy your visit! Maybe if things were different, maybe if one of you weren't about to leave the city for good, you could come here again sometime. Maybe this could become something special, something bigger than just a thing you tried once because, hey, why not? But on the other hand, it's probably best not to think about it too much. Just enjoy this for what it is. You've still got the boat ride back to Manhattan to look forward to, and if you load yourself up with too many might-have-beens, the ferry will sink under all that weight."

This area, New York, once called New Amsterdam by its early Dutch settlers and Lenapehoking by its native Algonquin peoples, is overflowing with its own half-buried past. The subway tunnels are nearly unnavigable, flooded by a thousand overlapping adventures. Should you, in your travels, zoom by the Lorimer stop on the L under Williamsburg, look closely at the swiftly passing platform and you'll see a young woman waiting, hair disheveled, makeup smeared—it's you during those six weeks when you would stumble home from Sean's apartment at three o'clock in the morning, high heels in hand, just because you didn't want to be one of those girls who spent the night.

The town is full of these triggers, and the longer you live here, the more land mines you set. There's the Gap at Astor Place, the bathroom at the Crocodile Lounge—the odds of stumbling into the lingering smoke of an old flame are staggering, and increasing still with every new significant instant spent with another significant other.

But of all the tributes to the fallen heroes and tragic victims of your fickle heart, a list as long and exhausting as a full avenue block, there remains one place more than any other you know you can never return to.

You know where it is and you go out of your way to not see it, to not be reminded of the thing that happened there. It's too much, this place. It would swallow you whole, this void, this pit, this unassuming two-story brownstone in Carroll Gardens that houses the one-bedroom apartment a much younger you and the man now listed in your phone as "DO NOT CALL HIM" were ever so foolish as to refer to as "home."

Sometimes you imagine DO NOT CALL HIM also not going there. You picture the two of you both not going there at the same time and not meeting each other outside on the sidewalk; you not taking the opportunity to tell him all the ways he wronged you, not explaining that even though you were over it now—so, so over it— you just wanted to make sure he didn't try that shit again with the next girl, for her sake.

"Because you're such a fucking humanitarian," he would not say, and you would wonder why you'd bothered to not meet up with him in the first place.

And then there's the Bronx, which is where people decide to get married—specifically the zoo part of the Bronx, specifically the part of the zoo that's in front of the Monkey House, and specifically your grandparents, who visited the Bronx Zoo Monkey House after six weeks of courtship and decided to get married.

"How did you make such a big decision after six weeks?" you once asked your grandmother. "You barely even knew each other."

"In those days, people didn't drag their feet so much. If you loved someone, you married him."

"But how did you know?"

"It was easy," she replied. "I asked your grandfather, 'Do you think we should get married?' And he said, 'Let's ask the monkeys. Hey, monkeys! You think we should get married?' And the monkeys were laughing, and he said, 'I think that's a yes.'"

"That's it? You got married because the monkeys were laughing?" Your grandmother shrugged. "I thought it was a sign."

You took Alex to the Bronx Zoo once—or was it Anthony?—to see if the primates might make some magic for you, but the Monkey House was gone. It had been torn down in 2012.

You decided that was a sign.

———

In Astoria, Queens, sits a small studio apartment in which

Carlos, love of your life for the moment, puts together his applications for grad school. During slow days at work or long rides on the N, you'll catch yourself daydreaming about Carlos getting accepted somewhere—and you following him—far, far away.

You imagine spending the rest of your life with this man, as you've imagined with all of them—not because you think you will necessarily, but just because you can't help but wonder.

You imagine the kids you'll have, the family vacations and anniversary dinners, the way you'll help each other with the dishes, the way you'll interrupt and editorialize each other's stories and jokes, the way you'll promise to never go to bed angry, even if that means—as it often will—staying up all night arguing.

But mostly, you imagine living somewhere else, miles and miles from this cramped and crowded once-thriving capital of the twentieth century. You could live in Austin, you think, or Minneapolis. You hear Seattle is gorgeous and you've never even been.

One morning, over breakfast and tea and the weekend *Seattle Times* in your spacious new downtown loft (or whatever kind of apartment people get in Seattle), Carlos will smile at you and you'll smile at him, and he'll scratch the back of his head in that shaggy Carlos way of his, and he'll say, "Hey, why don't we plan a trip to New York sometime? We can see a Broadway show, catch up with old friends . . ."

Carlos will clear the two cereal bowls, part of the brand-new set you bought when you moved here, and on the way to the sink, he'll kiss you gently on the forehead, the very forehead that's been so gently kissed by so many men, a marker amid thousands in a graveyard of kisses.

And you'll smile at this man and wonder if he too, like all those who came before him, will someday be a bittersweet memory, will someday be felled by the same foolish blunder of knowing you a little too well and yet also somehow not enough.

"What do you say? You want to go back to New York, see the sights?"

"No," you'll say. "There are too many ghosts there."

We Men of Science

My wife was eleven months pregnant at the time, which always seemed to me an awful lot of months to be pregnant.

Is that normal? I would say,

and Jessica would say: *The doctor says it's normal.*

and I would say: *I don't think it is.*

and she would say: *Are you a doctor, Yoni?*

and then I would say: *Yeah. I am, actually. So are you. Technically we are both doctors.*

and she would say: *Can we drop it?*

I earned my doctorate in aerospace engineering, but my real passion was always molecular biophysics. When I took the call from my friend and mentor, Dr. Carl Hesslein, I was in the middle of giving a lecture on the philosophy of science to a sparsely attended class of lazy sophomores who'd hoped my course might be an easy way to knock out a gen ed requirement at a mostly uninspiring and forgettable university. I don't mean to be rude about the school in question or its student body; those are just true statements.

I showed the class this slide:

(I drew it myself.)

First, the good news, I said: *We're doomed. Our planet is dying. Our universe is dying. Our friends, our family, everyone we've ever known, everyone we ever will know, all our distant progeny who are thousands of generations away from even being born, all of us, are slowly slowly dying dying dying.*

I showed this slide:

And then I said: *Oh, I'm sorry, did I say* GOOD *news?*

At this point, my lecture notes instructed me to: [PAUSE FOR LAUGHTER.]

Nobody laughed.

I paused anyway.

But there is *good news,* I continued. *And that is this: Science will live on after we're all dead. Science will survive with or without our attempts to understand it; science doesn't care.*

Like a callous ex-lover, science won't miss you, and sure, maybe that's a little scary, but isn't it also exciting?

My cell phone rang. I knew immediately it was Dr. Hesslein because of the ringtone, Beethoven's lush and haunting *Vienna on My Mind*.

I answered the phone: *Dr. Hesslein! I'm in class right now.*

The students continued to type into their laptops and phones. I entertained the idea that they were now taking notes on my personal phone call, but Occam's razor would suggest that they had never really been taking notes at all.

Carl spoke quickly in overlapping fragments, as if he, like science, had no particular desire to be understood: *Yoni! The grant! The board! Under the direction of! Was established! It's happening! I can't even! It's happening!*

The *it* that was *happening* was the Anti-Door, a project he and I both had spent the majority of our adult lives daydreaming about, all of a sudden becoming a reality thanks to a generous grant from the Frank and Felicity Fielding Foundation.

I first became interested in Carl's research several years earlier, after I witnessed Something Terrible on the Metro.

I was reading Milton Hilton's new book. It was a meditation on particle velocity levels—nothing revolutionary. Suddenly, very loudly, I heard Something Terrible happening.

No! Please don't!

I didn't look up.

Help, I heard. And then, just in case I hadn't heard: *Please help me. Please!*

I tried not to listen.

I focused on the words in my book. I read the same paragraph over and over again. This is what it said:

Particles, particles, everywhere particles. Also, Debra, I love you; will you marry me?

For dinner, Jessica and I had Chinese. My wife didn't like to cook—I say that like she should, like it's her job, excuse me—neither of us liked to cook. We got takeout a lot. That night we had Chinese.

I said: *How was your day?*

and she said: *Fucking fruit flies . . .*

and I said: *Yeah . . .*

She said: *How was* your *day?*

and I said: *Milton Hilton asked Debra to marry him.*

and she said: *That's nice.* And then: *Who's Debra?*

and I said: *I don't know.*

That night, I lay in bed and stared at the stars (we were remodeling at the time; our bedroom had no roof) and I thought about how I did nothing, how Something Terrible was happening and I did nothing, and I wondered if a better version of me might have acted less cowardly.

In the following days and months and years, I often pondered this un-me, an un-me who was gracious to my wife when I was callous and patient with my students when I was irritable. I thought about this man every time I meant to say *I love you* but instead I said *Don't touch that.* Every time I meant to say *YES!* but instead I said . . . *Yes?* Every time I meant to say *Everything's going to be okay* but instead I said nothing.

If I tell you I can't count all the times I've made the wrong call, chosen the wrong words, taken the wrong path, please know I'm not saying it to be modest about my counting skills, which I assure you are more than adequate. But if there was another me, an opposite, someone who did do all the right things—well, I figured, that guy could really be something.

Dr. Hesslein had written in detail about an anti-universe that counter-resembles our own, balancing us, neutralizing us, receiving our excess energy and converting it to anti-energy. The braver, wiser, better un-me would live there, as would the uns of everybody who ever existed. Everything the anti-universe is would fit neatly into the crevices of everything we are not, like two halves of an English muffin. It would have the solutions to our problems and it would inspire us to become a better un-them.

And now, having finally raised the capital, Dr. Hesslein was assembling a team of physicists and engineers to design and build the door that would take us there. He asked me whether I wanted to be a part of history if I wasn't too busy throwing words at handfuls of bored undergrads. I didn't even have to think about it.

Work began on the Anti-Door that fall, under the assumption that while we were constructing a door that opens in, scientists in the opposite universe would be building a corresponding door that opens out, because: logic.

My first day on the job, Jessica insisted on walking me to the Metro stop. She said: *Be careful with all those complex theoretical equations, okay? Some of them have sharp corners.*

and I said: *I'll be sure to wear gloves.*

For real, though, you're playing with the fundamentals of time and space. Don't create some sort of paradoxical pocket universe in which you were never born, because I still need you to clean the garage.

and I said: *Your concern is touching.*

and she said: *I was joking! I'm sorry; I'm nervous.*

and I said: *Don't be; it's bad for the baby.* I kissed her on the forehead.

She said: *Seriously, though, when you get back, you'll clean the garage?*

Of course, the universe is not black and white, and opposites turned out to be a little more fluid than we anticipated. The opposite of a dog can be a cat, or a different dog, or nothing at all, the absence of dog.

I should iterate that this is an oversimplification of the math, but it is emblematic of the basic principle. Here are a few more examples:

Ex:	Possible opposites
I will not go out today.	I [will] go out today.
	I will not [stay in] today.
	I [will] [stay in] today.
	I [will] [stay in] [every day].
My mother	[My father]
	[My wife]
	[My unborn child]
	[My mother] [(My mother is dead.)]
I don't say *I love you.*	I [say] *I love you.*
	I don't say [*I hate you*].
	[You] don't say [you love me].
	I don't say *I love you.* [I don't even think it.]

Note that in the last example, in three out of four cases, the opposite of silence is silence. We had announced with great fanfare a new
era of balance and understanding, but the more tests we ran, the less
certain we could be about what was on the other side of the door we
had just spent eight months building.

What if you walked through the Anti-Door and gravity lifted you
off the ground and hurled you into outer space? What if the oxygen
on the other side of the door was toxic? If there were no piranhas in
the room you left, would you walk into a roomful of piranhas? Or,
worst of all, what if the world on the other side of the door was no
better or worse than our own, just different? What if it was just as
heavy with war and famine and iniquity and cowardice?

But Frank and Felicity Fielding and their foundation were not
interested in what-ifs, they were interested in results, and since we
had none to offer, they cut funding, and I returned to the unglam-
orous life of being a minor annoyance for hungover teens, and a
husband, and eventually, presumably, a father.

One afternoon, after a particularly ill-received performance of my
lecture "Matter: Does It Matter?," I returned to my modest office on
the fourth floor of the science building to discover that the cramped,
poorly lit space the university had seen fit to give me was even more
overstuffed than usual.

Sitting in my chair with his feet up on the desk was Carl Hesslein,
and behind him, blocking the window facing the alley (the room's
sole source of natural light), stood the Anti-Door.

Why is this here? I asked,

and Dr. Hesslein said: *You think I was just going to hand this
over to FieldingCorp? They wouldn't even know what to do with it!*

and I said: We *don't even know what to do with it.*

and he said: *Just keep it here until I find a better hiding spot, okay?*

and I said: *But what if someone sees it? What if one of my students wants to visit during office hours?*

and he said: *Has that ever happened?*

and I said: *Not historically, no, but I like the idea that someone could surprise me.*

and he said: *Just keep it for a few weeks. I promise you'll forget it's even here.*

Well, I didn't forget. The door was behind me while I graded papers. The door was behind me while I ate lunches at my desk—a series of sad salads from the campus cafeteria. Every day, the room seemed smaller and the Anti-Door seemed larger.

It was behind me when I got a call from Jessica, after she went to see the doctor about the baby that wouldn't come out after a year and a half.

The doctor thinks it might be psychosomatic, she said. *He thinks maybe I subconsciously don't believe I'm ready for the baby.*

and I said: *Really? What do you think?*

and she said: *Well, I think I'm ready, but . . . maybe I'm sensing that* you're *not ready.*

What do you mean I'm not ready? I'm ready.

There was a pause, and she said: *I don't think you've really come to terms with the fact that everything's going to change once the baby gets here. Everything we were, our independent selves, our careers, all the things that mattered to us—*

and I said: *What makes you think I'm not ready for that?*

She sighed and said: *I don't know, Yoni.*

and I said: *I promise you the baby is going to come and it's going to be the most amazing thing that ever happened to us, and we are going to be wonderful parents, but until that happens, why don't we try to enjoy this extra time we have,* before *everything changes?*

and she said: *See, this is what I mean, about you not being ready.*

and I didn't say anything,

and she said: *I'm sorry, Yoni.*

and I said: *We'll talk about this when I get home.*

and she said: *Okay, Yoni.*

I hung up the phone, and the door was behind me

and I spun around to look at it,

and I rested my hand on the knob

and I turned the knob

and I opened the Anti-Door

and I walked through it.

As soon as I crossed the threshold I stumbled into a pool of water. I fell on all fours and spat up blood; I had swallowed a tooth. I squinted as my eyes adjusted to the new light. As far as I could tell, it was the same cramped office I had just come from, but with six inches of water in it. An incredibly handsome man in a dark blue corduroy coat was staring at me. I looked at the name on the office door.

You're Yonatan Beckerman, I said,

and he said: *No doyyyyyyy. I don't know how you got in my office, guy, but you wanna watch a video of me shooting hoops? I'm real skilled at shooting hoops.*

I said: *You're the opposite of me.*

and he said: *Shut up, you're the opposite of me.*

and I said: *Yes, both those things are true.*

and he said: *Shut up, neither of those things is true.*

and I thought: Jesus, this guy's a pain in the ass.

Then he said: *Hey, I don't know what your deal is, guy, but you want to come over for dinner? My wife's a really good cook; plus, she's a total babe.*

We walked to his house. The streets were flooded and the other Yonatan made fun of me for not bringing my boots. Everywhere, people were shouting and dropping large electronic appliances out windows. Horrifying bats fluttered from lamppost to lamppost.

Yonatan lived in a water-damaged mansion in the middle of a river. He kicked down the front door and shouted into the kitchen: *Jecka, I found this guy! He wants dinner.*

and I said: *My name is Yoni; I work at the university with your husband.*

The first thing I noticed about Jecka Beckerman was how very not pregnant she was. She wiped her hand on her apron and smiled widely as she offered it to me. *It's so nice to meet you,* she said. *Dinner will be ready in a minute.*

It was the best meal I'd had in years. Jecka told us about the research she'd been doing on four-winged hummingbirds. *Technically, they're not really birds,* she said. *We don't know what they are. But check out these migratory patterns . . .* I could barely follow her, she talked so quickly. She flitted wildly between ideas and knocked over several glasses of wine. *If the field test doesn't work, I'll die. I will actually literally fall over dead and stay dead for the rest of my life. But if it does work, oh, Yoni, if it does work . . . it's too good to say out loud.*

While Yonatan washed the dishes, I bored his wife with stories of my own career. At one point I must have reminded her of something else, because she bit her lower lip and said: *Do you like earthquakes?*

and I said: *Sure* (which is true). *Earthquakes, tornadoes, hurricanes—I like any situation where all of a sudden everything changes and the rules don't apply. I love an emergency.*

and Jecka said: *You want to know a secret? I do too.*

I walked back to Yonatan's campus, returned through the Anti-Door to my office, and took the Metro home. My wife was in the living room and I kissed her hard on the mouth and I said: *Hey, beautiful! Tell me something interesting about fruit flies.*

Jessica looked at me and said: *Yoni. They're fucking fruit flies.*

I started dipping into the world on the other side of the Anti-Door every day between classes, each time spitting out a new tooth and shoving it into my pocket so Jecka could sew it back into my mouth later. I became an expert at navigating my way through the opposite Beckermans' neighborhood and would try to beat my time from the campus to their house. Thirty minutes. Twenty minutes.

This new universe I had discovered was exciting and terrifying and romantic, as anything that's one tends to be all three. You walk through the Anti-Door, and suddenly you're a different person. Something is lost and something is gained. Something is forgotten and something is found. You reach into your pocket, you pull out a watch that wasn't there before, a photograph of a girl you don't recognize, the business card of a man you've never met.

On my birthday, Jecka baked me an earth-day-quake, a confectionary disaster littered with little green candy men diving for cover under a split cookie crust.

We sat together at one of Yonatan's basketball games. The court was on the top of a hill so they wouldn't have to play in the water. I leaned in close to the woman who was the opposite of my wife and whispered: *He's really very good.*

Jecka smiled. *Isn't he? I was going to make cupcakes, but . . . for some reason I didn't.*

I said: *That's okay; I can never eat cupcakes without feeling guilty.*

and she said: *Yonatan's the same way,* and I knew that one of us was lying.

I asked her about her field test. Her eyes sank and then flickered and she asked me what I was doing for New Year's. *Yonatan has to stay at the office and grade papers. Why don't you come over? I don't want to be alone.*

When I told Jessica I had to stay at the office and grade papers over New Year's, she took it harder than I expected.

Don't make me go to that party by myself, she said,

and I said: *You'll be fine.*

She said: *But guess what: I'm baking a pie. I never bake!*

and I said: *Save me a slice.*

Jessica used to say *guess what* a lot, because:

1. she thought it was cute, and
2. she was a scientist, and scientists (she claimed) should *always* be guessing what.

When she was in a playful mood, she would say: *Guess what, you are my husband, and guess what, I love you, and guess what, you are so adorable I just want to punch you in the face.*

and when she thought I needed cheering up, she would say: *Guess what.*

and I would say: *What?*

and she would say: *I think you're wonderful. And I am so proud of you.*

More often, however, she would use it as a rejoinder, as in: *Guess what, you forgot to do the dishes,* or: *Guess what, someone left his shoes in the middle of the living room for his pregnant wife to trip over.*

On New Year's, Jecka and I stood in the kitchen, drinking wine and listening to the radio (Yonatan had thrown the TV out the window). There was a war in some country that I was pretty sure didn't exist in my universe. Jecka leaned against the sink and bit her lower lip, which was something she often did right before asking me a question.

When did you know that you wanted to be a scientist? she asked, and I told her my "How I Became Interested in Science Story."

Yoni Beckerman's "How I Became Interested in Science Story"

When I was in fourth grade, Peter Weiss returned from a family vacation in Germany with a horrifying cough and a contagious fever that splattered across the class like a Jackson Pollock painting.

As it turned out, every single gentile in the class got sick. All the blond-haired Smiths and Vanderwilts disappeared, while the Rosenbergs and Cohens somehow seemed stronger, as if we were nourished by the absence of our classmates, like a garden suddenly free of weeds.

Eventually, doctors figured out that Peter Weiss got infected by residual toxins at a concentration camp he visited, and all the Jews in the class, grandchildren of survivors, had inherited DNA immunized due to years of exposure.

And that's when I realized that science is constantly happening all around us.

Every other subject is static: Brutus will have always betrayed Caesar, one and one will always make two, and when two vowels go a-walking, the first one will always do the talking. But in science, we're constantly making new discoveries.

We're the last pioneers.

Jecka looked at me and bit her lower lip, and I could tell she wanted to ask me something so I said: *What?*

and she said: *When you walk through the Anti-Door, does it make you happier?*

I'm always happy to see you, I said,

and she said: *Yeah, but I was thinking . . . Say I'm at one-third happiness. If I were to walk through the door, do I all of a sudden become two-thirds happy?*

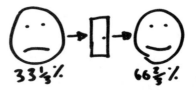

33⅓%   66⅔%

I guess so, I said. *Double your happiness!*

and she said: *But that's the problem; I don't know how happy I am. For all I know I could be at seventy-five percent happiness, and if I went through the door I'd suddenly get knocked down to twenty-five.*

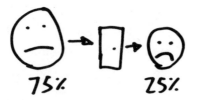

I don't know what would be sadder: that I would now be a third as happy as I was before, or the realization that what I was before—that is to say, what I am now—is three-quarters as happy as I could possibly get.

What if I was zero percent happy, and I walked through the door to find that a hundred percent happy still isn't all that happy?

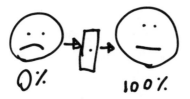

What then?

And I started to say: *That's not actually—* but she was really worked up and then all of a sudden it was almost midnight and I said: *Happy New—* and the second hand on my watch quivered and all of a sudden it was midnight and we were kissing. The people on the radio were cheering and I heard explosions in the distance, and I opened my eyes while I kissed her and I saw a four-winged hummingbird at the window and everything was too, too beautiful.

Then, all of a sudden, midnight was over and I felt deeply ashamed. It was midnight and one second, which is pretty much as far from midnight as you can get without going backward. I said: *Well, I should . . .*

and she said: *No, please. Stay with me. Just for a little bit.*

Perhaps a better me would have done the right thing and left, or a worse me wouldn't have worried about it, just indulged in the transgression, but I am only as good as I am, and I could only do what the person as good as I am could do.

A statue isn't built from the ground up—it's chiseled out of a block of marble—and I often wonder if we aren't likewise shaped by the qualities we lack, outlined by the empty space where the marble used to be. I'll be sitting on a train. I'll be lying awake in bed. I'll be watching a movie; I'll be laughing. And then, all of a sudden, I'll be struck by the paralyzing truth: It's not what we do that makes us who we are. It's what we don't do that defines us.

I took the Metro back to Yonatan's campus and slid my key into the door of his office. When I reentered my own universe, the room was flooded; I must have left the Anti-Door open. It was a long walk home. I crawled into bed, and Jessica was half awake and she whispered: *Hey.*

I said: *Hey there.*

She pointed to her cheek and I kissed her

and I asked: *How was the party?*

and she said: *Boring. I wish you'd been there.*

and I said: *I'm sorry.*

She said: *I can't talk to people. I have too many teeth in my mouth; all the words come out wrong. I keep growing new teeth—it's really weird. Do you think it could be a side effect of the pregnancy?*

and I said: *I don't know.*

We lay in bed and looked at the stars (we were fumigating the house; the bed was outside) and Jessica said: *I missed you.*

I said: *Have you ever wondered what it's like to go through the Anti-Door?*

and she mumbled: *Sometimes.*

and she fell asleep.

The next morning, my cell phone woke us up early and Jessica shouted: *Turn that fucking thing off!* It was Dr. Hesslein's assistant and the ringtone was Mahler's up-tempo march *My Baby Takes the Morning Ludwigsbahn.*

She said: *Yoni, it's Carl . . . he's dead.*

and I said: *Oh my God, is he okay?*

and she said: *Yeah, well, he's dead, so . . . no.*

Carl had left the faucet running in his house overnight. The whole building had filled up with water and he drowned in his sleep.

We went to the funeral and the shiva call. I said some very nice and accurate things. Jessica squeezed my hand lovingly. But the whole time, all I was thinking was: I have the Anti-Door in my office, and now nobody knows about it but me.

I visited Jecka more. We made love in the bed she shared with her husband, the opposite of the bed I shared with my wife, and since we were each the opposite of the other one's spouse, I allowed myself to be convinced—no, I convinced myself—that mathematically this was a neutral act.

One day, after performing a neutral act, I returned through the Anti-Door to my office. The room was now half full of water and

Dr. Hesslein was sitting on my desk, his feet on my chair, and he pointed at the door to the hallway and said: *Yoni! I want for this door to be by you hidden kept. Just until this happens, I will find a place worse.*

and I said: *This isn't right. This happened already. You're dead. In this universe you're dead.*

Dr. Hesslein nodded solemnly. *This was afraid I would happen.*

I also nodded solemnly, pretending I understood what he was talking about.

He grabbed a legal pad and doodled out a diagram. *I wouldn't be lying if I didn't say I wasn't concerned.* He paused, then concentrated on his words: *When I will leave the Anti-Door with you . . . No. When I* left *the Anti-Door with you, I was hoping you would use it. But I thought you could travel back and forth between universes, like a beam of light bouncing repeatedly between two parallel mirrors.*

Instead, you've fallen through them like a light hitting two mirrors at a diagonal, skipping across them infinitely. You understand? You don't come back to the same place you came from!

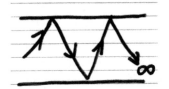

Wanting proof, I grabbed a familiar book: Milton Hilton. I turned to a page I knew well, the one where Hilton asked Debra to marry him. It now said:

Particles, particles, everywhere particles. Also, Debra, I love you, but I think I need to be alone for a little bit.

Things with Jecka got more complicated. The more I visited her, the more trouble we had communicating. She was depressed. She hated her husband. I would try to tell her: *Things will get better,* but it came out as: *Nothing didn't get worse.* One day, over takeout, she told me she didn't love me. I didn't know if she meant exactly that or the opposite. She told me she was pregnant. All I could say was WOW, which is MOM upside down.

I crossed the street and crawled through the Anti-Door. Dr. Hess-lein was standing on the ceiling of my office, crying and laughing at the same time. Tears were flowing up into his eyes. He shouted at me: *Yoni! Everything was always a mistake! You are so wonderfully unapologetic! Can you never not unforgive me?*

I spat out a tooth.

My house was so far away and it rained the whole walk back. Jessica was in the living room, glaring, horrified, at our newborn baby son. I said: *It's beautiful.*

She didn't say anything

so I said again: *He's beautiful.*

She said: *I can't stop cooking. I don't know why. I can't stop cooking food and I can't close my mouth because of all my teeth and I don't know what's happening to me and I don't know what's happening to us and I've never been more scared.*

I wanted to say: *Everything's going to be okay,* but instead what I said was nothing.

She said: *You're cheating on me.*

and I didn't say anything,

and she said: *That was a question. Are you cheating on me?*

and I didn't say anything,

and she said: *If you're cheating on me, don't say anything.*

and I didn't say anything.

Guess what, she said: *I hate you.*

and I said: *I probably could have guessed that.*

I almost left, she said: *I almost took the baby and left, but I love you too much.*

and I said: *You almost left?*

and she said: *Yeah, but I didn't.*

I ran for what felt like hours through the waterlogged streets, racing past overturned cars and disgusting birds and billboards advertising Milton Hilton's new book, *Debra, I'm Sorry, Please Take Me Back.*

My keys wouldn't unlock my office, so I kicked down the door and dove through the Anti-Door directly into the Beckermans' kitchen, where Yonatan was drinking milk and rum and staring at the wall.

What happened? I said,

and he held up a note: *I almost stayed. But I didn't.*

I sat next to him and neither of us said anything for a while.

I said: *Do you remember, several years ago, on the Metro . . .* I started over: *Did you ever witness Something Terrible?*

He nodded.

Did anything—I mean, how did you—I mean . . . I started over: *What did you do to stop it?*

He shook his head.

He had done nothing, just like me. He recalled the shouting, the fear—we recited in unison the passage of Milton Hilton that we had both read over and over. *Particles, particles, everywhere particles.* As near as we could figure out, the only thing different about his experience was that he didn't lie in bed awake wondering what his opposite would have done.

I thought again about what we used to say in the lab—how, as a general rule, the opposite of silence is silence.

I said: *What am I doing here?*

It was a rhetorical question, but I didn't give Yonatan much credit in the knowing-which-questions-are-rhetorical department, so I was surprised when he didn't answer.

There's an old joke my mother used to tell me, about a rabbi and his student:

What's purple, hangs on the wall, and sings? asks the rabbi,

and the student says: *I don't know. What's purple, hangs on the wall, and sings?*

and the rabbi answers: *A dead herring!*

But, Rabbi, a dead herring isn't purple.

Well, you could paint it purple.

But, Rabbi, a dead herring doesn't hang on the wall.

Well, you could hang it on the wall.

But, Rabbi, a dead herring definitely doesn't sing!

Oh, that? That I just threw in to confuse you!

[PAUSE FOR LAUGHTER.]

———

It occurred to me that maybe I'd tried to push the edges of my universe too far. After all, we live in the real world, and in the real world, you can paint a dead herring purple, and you can hang it on the wall, but hard as you try, you can't make it sing.

And I imagined that if I were in some other, better universe, there'd be someone who could tell me, *It's okay*, or *You'll get 'em next time, tiger*. Someone would tell me that all the stupid things I'd done, all my mistakes, they didn't matter. This someone would say that, no matter what, she was proud of me, that I filled her heart with warmth, and that that's really the most you could hope for in life—to just for an instant make somebody else just a little bit happier. She would tell me that—guess what!—everything was going to be all right.

But in this universe, there was just this empty room in this ugly house in this horrifying city, and there were two Yonatans there, and one of them turned to the other and said dully: *Do you want to shoot some hoops?*

We played a few games and I was better than I expected. He beat me, of course, but not by a lot. I stole the ball a couple times and surprised myself by completing a layup. At one point, we watched the sun set over the river and light up the horizon. Yonatan took it in, this wedge of transcendent beauty separating the ugly day and the terrifying night, and I got really lucky and scored a three-pointer while he was crying.

LIES WE TOLD EACH OTHER

(a partial list)

- You look really familiar; have I seen you somewhere before?
- I never have more than two (re: drinks).
- Funny story: I actually make a really good boyfriend.
- That's hilarious.
- That is so interesting.
- That is so funny.
- That's really funny.
- [laughter]
- I *really* never have more than five (re: drinks).
- I basically had a double major.
- I'm pretty much running the place.
- I know what you mean.
- Oh yeah, I think I read that somewhere.
- I love this song.
- *I* love this song!
- That is literally the craziest thing I've ever heard.
- I literally can't eat any more of this.
- I gotta get up early in the morning . . .
    - I have this thing for work . . .

- I'm sorry I haven't called you; things have been crazy.
- I can't on Friday. I have a thing on Friday.
  - Just some friends. Seeing some friends.
- I wrote this song in, like, five minutes. It's not very good.
- I honestly never think about him anymore (re: Blake).
- More than ten, but fewer than twenty (re: women).
- It's this dumb work party—if you don't want to go, I won't hold it against you.
- No, that sounds like a lot of fun.
- You were the handsomest guy there.
  - No, I'm serious.
- Yeah, they seem really cool (re: work friends).
- I . . . love you too.
- I've never felt like this before.
- This moment, right here, is the happiest moment of my life.
- Yes.
- Yeah.
- No.
- Definitely.
- I love them (re: earrings).
- It's delicious (re: soup).
- I just feel like we *get* each other in a way most couples don't.
- I also feel that way, exactly.
- I *was* listening.
- I didn't even notice her.
- Just a guy I work with.
- You're reading too much into things.
- He's like a brother!
  - It would just be weird.
- I've never thought of her in that way.

- Well, that's really wonderful.
  - No, I'm not being passive aggressive.
  - I really think it's wonderful.
  - I don't know what "tone" you're talking about.
    - I'm telling you it's wonderful.
- I love your friends.
  - You know I love your friends.
- What are you talking about? You're great at parties.
- I didn't notice (re: weight gain).
  - No, I'm telling you, you look exactly the same to me.
- I told you red (re: wine).
  - I definitely said red.
- I checked the weather before we left.
- I didn't see your text until I was already on my way home.
- They want it to be just the guys, no girlfriends.
  - I think it's stupid, personally, but what can you do?
  - I'll tell them you said that.
- You don't need to apologize to me.
- I think the most important thing is honesty.
- It's fine.
- Fine.
- It's really fine.
  - I told you it's fine.
- I'm fine.
- Of course I'm happy for you (re: promotion)!
  - I'm thrilled!
- I can listen and check my emails at the same time.
- I don't keep track of those things the way you do (re: who "won" argument).
- I do trust you (re: Blake).

- Okay, you're right.
  - I am not just saying that so you'll shut up, do you know how degrading that is?
- She seems really nice.
  - I like her.
- It doesn't bother me.
- Just do whatever you want; I don't have an opinion one way or the other.
- It was just coffee!
- I think you're overreacting.
- I'm sorry.
- I had to work late.
  - I told you, I was at work.
  - Why would I lie about being at work? I don't understand you.
  - I actually have no idea what you're talking about.
    - I really don't.
      - Truly.
  - This? Whatever this is? It's all in your head.
- You don't know me at all.
- I didn't mean it like that.
- I don't deserve this.
- I'm just thinking, what's going to be best for *you*?
- All I want is for you to be happy.
  - That's *all* I want.
- I think maybe the problem is I love you *too* much. Could that be the problem?
- Once everything settles down at work, things will get easier with us.
- If you would just come home, we could talk about this like adults.

- That is so mean; I do *not* have one foot out the door.
- Damn it, we can make this work.
  - I want to make this work.
  - I am *dedicated* to making this work.
- I actually think that fight was a really good fight for us, as a couple.
- I am never going to hurt you like that again.
- I love you.
- I love you too.

These Are
Facts

West fucked his foot up real bad his first day on the beach. God fucking damn it, and of course this would happen, and what a way to start the fucking week.

It's not even as if he was doing anything really; he was just fucking standing there, just chilling knee-deep in the water and trying to take it easy like a real honest-to-God person on vacation would. He was just starting to get comfortable, for like maybe the first time in his whole fucking life, when a rogue wave poured some rocks and shells and probably even some broken glass right onto his foot and scraped it up something ridiculous, covering it in all sorts of bruises and bumps so that it looked like a topographical map of God knows what, each gash and cut representing a river or a tributary or a mountain range or whatever the fuck they've got on topographical maps these days.

This was Friday, or, as they called it in Puerto Vallarta, "Friday," because everyone at the resort spoke English. West didn't even attempt to pull out any of his eight-years-rusty high school Spanish, although sometimes after the bartender gave him *una cerveza*, he would say, *"Merci beaucoup,"* because that was his idea of a real funny joke. It was funny because the bartenders all spoke English anyway and—you know what, if he has to explain it to you, it's not even worth it.

The good news was that even with a fucked-up foot, West could still do what he really wanted to do, which was sit on the beach and drink beers all day and look at the water. In fact, the foot was a blessing in disguise, because it meant he didn't have to do anything he didn't want to. His father or his father's current wife would say, "Hey, you want to go into town?" or "You want to look at some ruins?" or "You want to go on a boat?" And West would wince and say, "Yeah, I'd really love to, but . . . the foot."

It was a conversation piece really; good-looking American *chicas* could come up to him and say, "Hey, what happened to your foot?" And he could respond, "Better question: What happened to our society to make it so we view damaged things as somehow incomplete? On the contrary, I, for one, believe it is our damage that makes us whole." And then he could have sex with them.

Of course that never actually happened, not while you were there, but as West told you repeatedly, that's just because you were there. "No girl's going to come up and talk to me when I've got another girl sitting right next to me. I mean, that's just common sense." You would ask him if he wanted you to leave, and West would shrug and say, "It's a free country," and then, remembering he was in Mexico, he would add, "Wait. It is, right?"

You didn't get to the resort until Saturday. You told your parents you couldn't fly out with them on Friday because Friday was Meaghan Doherty's graduation party, but in fact, you didn't go to Meaghan's party. You stayed home. You drew a bath for yourself, which at the time felt so sophisticated and adult. As a child, you often took baths, but this time you *drew* a bath, a bath was *drawn,* and as if that weren't enough, you lit a candle (a candle!) and you pulled your parents' turntable into the bathroom and played a Joni Mitchell record (which one, it doesn't matter—it was *Blue*—it doesn't matter), and you laugh about it now, but at the time it all felt so significant. You were done with high school forever, and soon they would ship you off to college in Boston, where you would forget about all the friends and enemies you had in high school, all the things that were so important, all the inside jokes.

Every seven years, the cells in our bodies completely replace themselves and we become entirely different people. Sitting in the bath, listening to "California," you thought about your temporary cells and you thought about how one day you would change; you would wake up one morning and all of a sudden everything would be different and all the things that used to make you cry would make you roll your eyes and all the things that used to make you roll your eyes would make you cry. But, of course, that would all be many, many years from now.

Incidentally, that thing about the new cells every seven years? This was a FACT, and if you looked you could find it somewhere in your private book of facts you shared with no one—a spiral-bound blue notebook upon whose first page you wrote in shaky calligraphy, "These Are Facts," and between whose covers hid hundreds of secrets as mundane and true as "FACT: Killer whales aren't really whales; they're dolphins."

Your half brother volunteered to meet you at the airport on Saturday. Your mom thought the whole family should go, but your father convinced her that you kids could use some catching up time. After all, how long had it been? After all, wasn't that the whole point?

West scrawled HEATHER in big block letters on a yellow legal pad and held the sign up at baggage claim, where he waited for your arrival. It was eighty percent as a joke, the sign, but twenty percent because he was actually a little worried he wouldn't recognize you, it had been so long.

After collecting your luggage and going through customs, you saw him: a very hairy hodgepodge of a person, in cargo shorts and aviator sunglasses and an inexplicably long-sleeved T-shirt, as if it weren't about a hundred degrees outside. Limping back and forth and picking at his beard, this mysterious other progeny of your father's looked somehow both older and younger than his own twenty-six years. FACT: He kind of looked like a homeless person.

"Look at you," West said.

And you said, "Look at *you.*"

And West said, "No. Look at you, man. Just fucking look at you."

Flying West out to Puerto Vallarta was your mother's idea. You had heard your parents arguing about it through the bedroom wall.

"This is supposed to be a vacation," your father said. "I love West, but you know he's going to be a pain in the ass all week."

"I want Heather to know her brother."

And here he was, this scrawny swizzle stick of a dude, carrying your luggage from the elevator to the room. It was almost too much, to see him again after all these years. Just the smell of him, it was almost too much.

"I took the bed by the bathroom; I hope that's okay. I figured you might want to sleep by the window."

"Some view," you said. Your room looked out over a construction site. The Crown Imperial was expanding. A crane was lifting a girder, moving it from one pile of girders to another pile of girders. One day, all this would be resort.

West frowned and shifted his weight uncomfortably. "This room's pretty bougie; it stresses me out. You want to get down to the beach, get a drink? Oh, shit, you probably want to see your parents, huh?"

You shrugged. "I see them all the time. This is supposed to be a vacation, right?"

West thought that was hilarious.

You found a pair of deck chairs in the sand under a big wooden umbrella and threw a towel over one of them. Your sort-of brother grabbed a roaming hotel waiter and ordered two beers and a banana daiquiri. "They really try to sell you on the pineapple drinks," he said, "but I figured out that they make the pineapple drinks from like a sludge and the banana drinks use real bananas."

"Oh, I don't drink," you blurted out, as if he had asked you, as if anybody cared.

"Oh, good," West said a little too loudly. He winked at you (why?), then said to the waiter, "A virgin daiquiri for the lady," grinning warmly, like it was some private joke the two of them shared.

"You probably don't remember me at all," West said, lighting a cigarette. "What were you, like six?"

You nodded. You didn't remember him, not really, and what you did remember you weren't sure if you actually remembered it or if you'd just invented it, cobbled together a brother from the elliptical stories your parents told and the worried glances they'd share whenever his name came up.

"Shouting," you said. "I remember a lot of shouting."

"Yeah," he laughed. "Me too."

You squinted at the sun bouncing off the water. "You want to go in the ocean?"

"Nah, you go ahead," he said, between drags of his cigarette. "I'll watch."

And you did.

And he did.

You met your parents for dinner at the hotel restaurant.

"It looks like you already got some sun, Heather," your dad said. "I hope you were wearing sunscreen . . ."

"How's your foot?" your mom asked.

And West answered, "Well, it's fucked, June."

Your dad crossed his arms and said, "Should we ask the front desk to call a doctor?"

And West said, "No, Dad, I'll be fine, but your display of paternal compassion has been noted by all."

Your mother frowned sympathetically. "Well, hopefully it doesn't ruin the whole trip for you."

After dinner, you walked your mom back to her room. She held your hand and smiled at you warmly, and you privately wondered how many times in the next few months before you left for college she would hold your hand and smile at you warmly.

"You don't mind sharing a room with West, do you?"

And you said, "No, Mom," like it was nothing. Like why would she even have to ask?

You washed your face and got into bed. You pulled a book out of your bag.

"What are you reading?" West asked.

"Oh, it's just this dumb book about these high school girls in New York."

"Is it any good?"

You blushed. "No, but I want to know what happens."

"Well, I'm bored," he said. "I'm going to go downstairs, get a drink. You want to come?"

At the resort bar, West regaled you with tales of adventure: the time he found a whole room's worth of furniture just lying by the side of the road; the party he crashed where he had sex with that guitar player's girlfriend; the time he got bedbugs somehow. When he felt the bar was getting "really bougie all of a sudden," he took you out for a limp along the beach.

"So, bring me up to the present. You got a boyfriend?"

You shook your head.

"Why not? You're a good-looking girl."

"I don't know," you said. "I feel like there were guys who wanted me to be their girlfriend. I just never met a guy who I thought was worth it."

"Worth what?" West asked, and you shrugged.

"I don't know. It. All of it."

"I actually think that's the right idea," he said. "Take your time. A lot of teens these days are too eager to grow up."

You laughed. "Oh yeah? Is that a true fact about teens?"

He smiled self-consciously. "I don't know; you're the teen, you tell me."

"I guess you're right," you said. "But I don't think that like being in relationships and having sex is necessarily the same thing as growing up, you know? Like 'growing up' can mean a lot of things."

"See, now that's an astute observation—and it also tells me why you never had a boyfriend."

"What's that supposed to mean?"

"You're too smart for high school boys. You must have gotten your smarts from your mom's side."

"Must have," you said. "Definitely didn't get it from my dad, the clinical psychologist."

"Naw, don't be fooled by his fancy job, Heather; I promise you that asshole's as dumb as they come."

For a moment, you debated whether to poke at this open sore, and then you wondered if your desire to poke at open sores was something you got from your dad, the clinical psychologist.

Then West said, "What the fuck is that thing?"

You looked up. About ten yards down the beach was a dog, some sort of terrier mutt, flinching and panting in the sand. West raced ahead to get a better look.

"Oh shit."

"Is he okay?"

"Hey, are you all right, guy?"

The dog whimpered.

"Shit. This dog is super-fucked-up. I think it's like having a seizure or some shit."

"Well, don't touch it," you said as West scooped the dog up into his arms and started limping back toward the resort. "Be careful," you shouted. "That dog could have rabies or something!"

You followed your brother through the lobby of the Crown Imperial.

"Sir, you can't bring that animal in here. Sir? Please!"

West dumped the dog on the front desk. "We found this guy on the beach; I think he's really hurt," he said. "You gotta do something."

The dog had stopped shaking and was now just lying on the counter, whimpering and drooling. And the concierge said, "Sir? Sir!"

And West said, "Don't fucking 'sir' me. This dog needs medical fucking attention."

And the man asked, "Is this your dog?"

West threw his arms up and paced an angry little circle. "No, it's not my dog. I told you. Does anyone here speak fucking English?"

People were starting to stare. A group of fratty-looking college guys. An older couple. A man with his kid.

You said, "Calm down, West," and the concierge looked at you and said, "Can you please tell him to calm down?" as if you hadn't just done exactly that.

"Is there like a dog doctor you can call? Does Mexico have fucking animal doctors or what?"

The concierge was trying to stay calm himself: "Sir, the hotel has a policy—"

West shouted, "Can you give him some fucking water or something at least? Jesus Christ."

Now the man with the kid was yelling, "Hey, why don't you watch your language, huh?"

"Watch my language? This dog is going to fucking die!" Then immediately: "I'm sorry. You're right. I'm sorry about the language."

By now, the concierge's boss had come out and he said, "Sir, we have called animal services. They are on their way. Would you like to wait for them with the animal?"

West exhaled. "Yeah. Thanks a lot, I really appreciate it."

"Okay, but he can't stay in here. We'll move him out front, okay?"

"Yeah. Hey, look, I'm sorry about before, when I said does anyone here speak English."

"It's okay."

"Everyone speaks English great here. But you shouldn't have to; it's your country. But everyone speaks English great. I was being a dick, in the heat of the moment, you know?"

The man shook his head. "I understand you are upset. It's not a problem, sir."

West looked at his name tag. "Jorge? You're a fucking stand-up guy; don't let anyone tell you any different."

Jorge nodded. "Okay, sir."

Two hotel employees carefully wrapped the dog in a Crown Imperial towel and carried him toward the front entrance. You followed them out and passed the man with the kid.

"Hey, listen," the man said. "I know you're really upset about the dog, but this is a family resort. You think you could do me a favor and go easy on the cuss words?"

"Yeah, I know," West said. "Sorry. I'm just—fuck! Sorry. I'm sorry."

The two bellhops laid the dog out on the steps in front of the building. West sat next to it and scratched its stomach.

"Hang in there, buddy," he said. He looked at you. "Are you cold?"

You shook your head. You weren't, not really.

A cab pulled up and a couple flailed out, drunk. "Oh my God, is that your dog?" the woman asked, and her husband said, "Come on, Amy, keep walking."

West shook his head.

"Is he okay?" Amy asked.

West said, "He's just tired."

Amy's husband ushered her into the Crown Imperial, and as they walked inside, you could hear Amy giggle, "I was like, why does that guy have a dog?"

West fiddled with an unlit cigarette.

"Hell of a first night," you said. He looked at you and you offered him a sad smile, but he didn't smile back.

"This is the worst," he said, his eyes all red. "This is the fucking worst."

FACT: On Sunday, West started drinking early. You spent the whole day with him, pretty much, just sitting on the beach, staring at the water.

At one point, your mom came by and asked if she could join you, and West said, "Yeah, I don't know, June, it's pretty crowded over here. You might have better luck by the pool."

And she said, "Okay, I can take a hint," and walked away, smiling tightly.

West looked at you and winced. "You must think I'm a real asshole."

And you did, kind of, but also: "No, I get it."

"It's not even her really. It's *him* that pisses me off."

"Sure, that makes sense," you lied. It did not make sense. FACT: Your father was the kindest, most conflict-averse person you knew, and it was hard to imagine him pissing *anybody* off. Sometimes, when he got overcharged at a restaurant, he'd pay the full bill, just because he'd rather spend the money than have to get into an argument.

"I mean, what Dad did to me and my mom . . . you can't just paper over that shit with a free trip to Mexico."

"What did he do?"

"He was an asshole, is what he did."

"No, but specifically . . ."

"People outgrow me," he said, in the same blasé tone one might say, "That is a tall building." He picked up a stick and chucked it into the water. "Everyone who ever loves me one day outgrows me."

It was unclear whether he was answering your question or trying to change the subject, but either way you felt like you should say something, so you said, "I won't outgrow you."

And he said, "Yeah, you will, because if you don't, that just means you're as fucked-up in the brain as I am." And he chuckled softly to himself and he looked over at you and gave you a crooked smile, the kind of crooked smile you'd previously seen only on your father and yourself, and in that moment your heart just about melted and FACT: You had never in your life wanted anything as much as you now wanted to be, immediately and forever, as fucked-up in the brain as your brother was.

"Why don't you take your shirt off at the beach?" you asked.

West shook his head. "I burn real easy. I get super-pink."

"Did you know flamingos get pink because of the food they eat? They eat a lot of shrimp, which makes their feathers grow in like that."

"Huh?" West spun his head to look at you, violently confused. "Oh, shit. Is this because I said you were smart last night, and now you have to like be the smart one all the time? You know, that's the problem with teenagers—you decide what you are, and then like you can't *be* anything else."

"No, that's not—"

"That exact mentality fucked me up when I was a kid, because I convinced myself I was an alcoholic—so for like five years, I never drank, or if I did drink I drank a *lot,* you know, because if I was already drinking, I might as well be 'that guy' that everyone already thought I was, but then one day, I was just like, 'What the fuck am I doing?' And now I just drink and it's not a big deal, you know?"

And you said, "I'm sorry. I just really like facts."

"Oh yeah?" West squinted at you over his sunglasses and you found new corners of yourself to sink into. He took a final drag off his cigarette and threw the butt in the sand. "I've got a fact for you. You know elephants?"

And you said, "Yeah," as if he were actually asking whether you knew what elephants were.

"Well, elephants have really sensitive feet, did you know that?"

You shook your head.

"They can feel things coming from miles away. They can feel a stampede or whatever from the vibrations in the ground, and they actually communicate with each other that way, from like way the hell off, through vibrations in the ground. I like to think about that whenever I'm far away from people. You know, it's like whenever you get lost, just remember to keep your feet on the ground."

"That's really nice," you said, "but I don't believe you."

And he laughed and said, "Why not?"

You took a sip from your virgin daiquiri and said, "I think you're a liar."

"Let's ask her," West said, nodding at a skinny but wide-hipped girl in a red-and-white-striped two-piece, walking along the beach.

You'd noticed the skinny but wide-hipped girl at the resort before. The previous night at the bar, she sat by herself at a nearby table while West gave you a lecture on early-nineties grunge music. You could feel her looking at you—you could feel her trying not to look at you—and you felt like how Erin Tyler must have felt at that sleepover party when she told the story about visiting her cousin in San Francisco during Fleet Week and letting the sailor touch her breasts in the parking lot of the Whole Foods. The event itself was not all that exciting or romantic, but you'd never know it from the giggling envy it brought out in the other girls. You'd wished those other girls could see you with West, wished they could trade places with the skinny but wide-hipped girl and see you holding court with this man eight years your senior, this overflowing mess of an adult.

And now the skinny but wide-hipped girl was walking past you and very obviously (to you, at least) trying not to betray how desperately she wanted to be invited into your private club. West got up and jogged toward her, forgetting apparently how much his foot was supposed to hurt, and you shouted, laughing, "Don't talk to him; he's a liar!"

West said to the girl, "Can I talk to you for a minute?"

"I heard you're a liar," she said.

And he shrugged and said, "That's a risk you'll have to take. Hey, how old are you anyway?"

"How *old* am I?"

"Yeah, I mean, don't you know?"

And she sized him up and said, "I'm eighteen."

And West said, "Great. That's perfect."

Her name was Jordan. She was visiting from Denver with her grandparents and her twin younger brothers she affectionately(?) referred to as the "Booger Patrol." She had a boyfriend back home, Clark, and she had never heard the thing about the elephants' feet.

"I swear to God I thought there was no one at the resort my age," she said to West, even though you were the one there who was her age. "I've been going up and down the beach; everyone here is either a little kid or an old man."

You tried to place Jordan, using the girls from your high school as references. She was a little bit Katie Connor, with Stephanie Pierson's nervous laugh and Sara Stone's seeming inability to shut up about starting at Northwestern in the fall.

"Northwestern's perfect for me because it's like in the city, but it's not *in the city* in the city, so you kind of get the best of both worlds."

West rolled his eyes and took a drag from his cigarette. "Cool. Have a great time in college."

"What's wrong with college?" Jordan asked.

He shook his head. "Nothing. A lot of really rich and outwardly successful people went to college."

You found that stupidly hilarious and you let out a surprised chortle. You weren't sure if you were laughing at him or laughing at her, but you knew they didn't know either, and you found that fact even more weirdly hilarious.

And when West left to take a leak in the ocean (because "those kids are just asking to get peed on"), Jordan said, "What's the story with your stepbrother?"

And you said, "What's his *story*?"

And she said, "Yeah, I mean, is he always like that?"

And you said, "Actually, West is my half brother."

And she said, "Oh. Sorry."

Monday you spent on the beach.

Jordan found you after breakfast. "The Booger Patrol was being a real pain in the ass this morning," she said, opening a Corona.

"Yeah," West said. "Little siblings are the worst," and he winked at you.

Jordan squinted at the horizon. "Do you want to go in the water?"

"Yeah," you said.

"You two go," said West. "I'll watch."

Jordan ran ahead and dove into a wave; you waded in after her. "Don't splash me," you said, and then immediately felt stupid. "I mean, don't splash me on purpose."

Jordan dunked her head and popped back up. "Did you see those college guys that are staying here? What's their story?"

You shrugged. "I think they're in a frat or something."

She nodded thoughtfully, taking in the information and mulling it over like the key to some puzzle. "Some of them are pretty cute. We should set you up with one."

"I don't know. They seem kind of dumb."

Jordan cackled. "Yeah, but it's not like you're going to marry them. If they're dumb, that's actually even better, because you'll spend less time talking and more time hooking up."

You looked back at the shore. West, true to his word, was watching you.

"Besides," she said, "I already have a boyfriend, so I have to live vicariously through you."

On Tuesday, the family went zip-lining. West declined, because his foot was still sore, but even if it wasn't, he wouldn't have gone, because a) fuck that noise, and b) are you fucking kidding me? The excursion was fun but cheesy. This was the jungle where they filmed *Predator*, a plaque explained, so all the zip lines were named after Arnold Schwarzenegger movies.

As for West, he mostly just fucked around on the beach, not that it's any of your business. Did Jordan come by? Yeah, she might've, a lot of people came by, who gives a shit?

He met up with you and your parents for dinner, at a place in town your mother had heard was "very authentic." The food was good, but you just about died from embarrassment when your mother kept trying to order in Spanish.

After the waiter left, you leaned in and whispered, "Mom. That guy probably speaks better English than you do."

"Well, I'm here in Mexico; I want to practice my Spanish."

"You can't just talk to Mexicans in Spanish; it's racist."

Your father rolled his eyes. "Oh, come on, how is it racist?"

"It just feels kind of racist," you said.

"She's right, June," said West, mouth full of beans. "It's super-racist."

And your mother said, "If we were in Paris, I would be speaking to the waiters in French."

"Yeah, but that's different."

"How is that different?" said your father.

You weren't sure. "It just—it feels like you're being condescending."

And your father said, "I think you're bringing some assumptions to the table that are unfair."

West turned toward you. "He's got a good point. Maybe you're the one being racist," he said, mouth full of beans.

Your waiter returned to the table, and your mother said, "Sergio? Did it make you uncomfortable, when I spoke to you in Spanish earlier?"

Sergio's face got very serious. "Uncomfortable? No."

"Would you rather customers speak to you in English?"

"English, Spanish, it's all okay. No problem either way."

After the meal, your mom wanted to see the History Show, this circusy spectacular in a nearby village.

West leaned back. "Yeah, I'm kinda not really into all that touristy bullshit."

And your dad said, "Oh, because sitting on the beach and drinking cocktails isn't touristy?"

And West let out a single cackle—"Ha!"—and then said, "No, but seriously, I don't want to go to any dumbass History Show."

"I'm kind of exhausted after the zip-lining," you said. "Maybe I'll stick around the resort with West."

Your mother shot your dad a glance, but he didn't even notice. "Are you sure, honey?" she said. "The show actually doesn't seem that touristy, the way the brochure describes it. I think it could actually be a really genuine cultural experience."

West said, "No means no, June. Give it a rest."

And you said, "Actually, you know what, maybe I will go."

It was a big arena show with a cast of hundreds in an old wooden stadium. The whole thing was in Spanish, but it was pretty easy to make out what was going on—a breathless rundown of everything that had ever happened, from the Mayans and other early settlers all the way up to the present. It wasn't bad. You were glad you went. Your mom seemed happy you were there, so even just for that.

On the cab ride back to the Crown Imperial, you thought about what it would be like to grow up in Puerto Vallarta. You imagined yourself going to the History Show as a Mexican child—it was something every kid did, like how kids in the U.S. go to Six Flags or the Holocaust museum. You'd go all the time; you'd practically have the whole thing memorized. You imagined going back, one last time, before you left for college.

"Come on, Elena," you'd say to your beautiful and glamorous Mexican best friend. "It'll be fun."

And she'd say, "The History Show? Are you kidding me?"

The two of you would sit in the back and make jokes the whole time. "Oh, so now the Aztecs and the Spaniards are friends? Yeah, that's *exactly* how it happened." At the end of the night, though, when the lights lit up the stage like the Mexican flag and the entire audience was singing, you'd shut up.

After the show, your mother would ask you where you'd been. "Elena and I went to the History Show."

She wouldn't get that you did it kind of as a joke and kind of for real, the way eighteen-year-olds do everything, and she would hold you close and whisper in your ear, "Oh, Heather"—or whatever the Spanish equivalent of Heather is—"promise me you'll never forget who you are."

As you were falling asleep that night, you thought about your imaginary best friend Elena and your imaginary Mexican mother and how neither could quite understand what was so poignant to you about the Mexican History Show. And you thought about how even though this scenario was made up, there was something so truthful about it because FACT: The things that are the most important aren't shared; they are important only to us.

The way your mother rolls her eyes at you, your sudden decision to stop eating red meat, the immediate unexplainable sadness you felt when you saw your father's shirt draped over the back of a chair. You can write it all down, you can put it in your book of facts, but the truth is no one can ever really understand the tangle of experiences and passions that makes you who you are. It's a secret collection, a private language, a pebble in your pocket that you play with when you're anxious, hard as geometry, smooth as soap.

Even a kiss between two people, stolen backstage on the opening night of your middle school's production of *The Music Man*. Peeking through the curtains, Harold Hill whispered to you, the Mayor's Wife, "I'm so nervous." And then he said, "We're going to remember this moment forever, aren't we?" And before you could answer, he kissed you quickly and softly on the mouth—he kissed you so gently, as if you were a paper crane, as if you were a creature made of tissue that would fall apart in the wind. And afterward he looked at you, and then he whispered, "Oh."

Even that shared experience—its true significance anyway, what it really means—that belongs to you alone.

"Shh, you're going to wake up Heather." It was Jordan who said this, in your hotel room, waking you briefly in the middle of the night, but when she did, you couldn't understand how that was possible. You were positive you must have dreamed it.

———

You woke up on Wednesday and the shower was running. West was in his bed, and you were in your bed, and the shower was running. There was a bra on the floor, and it wasn't your bra, and some clothes, and a clutch, and West was asleep in a long-sleeved T-shirt and the shower was running, and you got up and walked over to the bathroom, and the shower stopped, and Jordan walked out in a towel and smiled at you and whispered, "Hey."

"Why are you here?" you said, and she offered you a cartoon grimace and said, "Sorry, awkward."

And you said, "No. Why are you here, Jordan?"

"I don't know, we were having fun last night, and West asked if I wanted to come back up to the room and I said yes. Where were you last night?"

"What about Clark?" you said, and she said, "I know, I feel kind of bad about that, but we're probably going to break up when I get to Northwestern anyway. And besides, it's not like I *cheated* on him. West and I didn't *do* anything. We just cuddled, and kissed a little bit."

When she said this, you must have made some face, because then she said, "I don't know why you're giving me a hard time about this. West and I have a *real connection*. I'm sorry if that makes you jealous or whatever because you have some weird crush on him."

And you said, "Ew, he's my brother," and she said, "Yeah, exactly, ew."

And you said, "I can't—I'm not—"

And West grunted and rolled over and looked up at the two of you in the doorway and kind of smiled and winced at the same time and said, "Well, if it isn't my two favorite ladies."

At this point you knew that if you didn't leave the room immediately you might accidentally/on purpose claw someone's eyes out, so you grabbed your key card and went down to the dining room. You met your mother down there, who frowned when she saw you and said, "You really should change out of your pajamas before coming down to breakfast."

That morning, you went snorkeling with your father (West had already politely declined the invitation), and in the afternoon you and your parents took a two-hour bus ride to look at some ruins.

How were the ruins? They were adequately ruined. Everything was ruined. "You're on your own for dinner," your mother said, and you had a burrito at the poolside café.

That night, West didn't come back to the room. You read your dumb book about high school girls in New York. It was stupid and dumb, but you wanted to know what happened.

On Thursday you had a plan.

Jordan would be gone on an all-day boat excursion with her grandparents and the Booger Patrol, so you'd have West all to yourself. You'd sit with West on the beach just like everything was normal, only everything wasn't normal, and he would know it.

West would try to cut the tension by saying something dumb, and then you would say something smart and West would try to deflect this by saying something like, "Tch . . ." or "Psh . . ." And you wouldn't let it rest, you would say, "Oh yeah? Psh?" And West would groan and say, "It's too early. I'm not drunk enough to be charming." And you would say, "You're not charming enough to be a drunk." And West would frown and say something ridiculous like, "You shouldn't be so clever, it's bad for your skin." And you would just take a sip from your daiquiri and say, *"Okay,"* in a tone all at once off-the-cuff and demolishing. And that would really make him feel stupid. That would just about destroy him.

FACT: You didn't see West all day Thursday.

At one point, your father found you reading your book by the side of the pool and said, "Where's West?"

And you shrugged and mumbled, "How should I know? I barely even know the guy."

And your father said, "Okay."

He started to walk away, but then you said, "And by the way, it is supremely weird that you would make me share a room with this twenty-six-year-old man I don't know."

And your father said, "Come on. You know West. You grew up with him."

"He moved out when I was six."

Your father rolled his eyes. "So you want your own room, like you have at home? Is that what this is about?"

"No, Dad—"

"Because lots of people share rooms with their siblings. I shared a room with my sister until I went to college—"

"No, it's not about that. I just think it's kind of fucked-up that this vacation is the first time I'm meeting him."

"It's not the first—"

"The first time since I was six."

"First of all, please watch your language," he said. "Second of all, what you might not understand is that West has done a lot of grow-ing up in the last ten years. Your mother and I did what was best for you. If you'd gotten to know him when you were younger, I don't think you would have liked him very much."

And you said, "Yeah, well, I hardly like him now."

"Well, I'm sorry you feel that way, but you're not getting your own room. These rooms are very expensive."

FACT: Your father was kind of an asshole.

Friday morning, you woke up to find West lying facedown in his bed in a pair of boxer shorts and a long-sleeved T-shirt, the sheet half off the mattress. You were going to leave without saying anything, because honestly, what was there to say?

But then he flopped around on the bed, and you couldn't tell if he was waking up or if it was just like gas escaping from a bloated corpse. And like a sick thing looking for a place to die, the question crawled out of his mouth: "Are you coming to the beach today?"

And you said, "Where have you been?" You tried to sound casual when you said it and then immediately hated yourself for trying to sound casual. As if you owed him that.

And he groaned, "You know, around. Come to the beach."

"Is Jordan going to be there?"

"Jesus, I don't know."

And you said, "Where have you been?" but this time you said it really seriously, so he would know that you were really serious.

And he said, "What, just because we hung out for a couple days, now we gotta do everything together?"

And you said, "What is your deal? Why did you even come here?"

And he said, "I came here to sit on the beach and get drunk. Why did *you* come here?"

And you said, "I came here to see you."

You thought that would shut him up, but you were starting to discover, FACT: The men in your family didn't shut up.

"Oh, really? Is that why you keep going on little outings with your parents?"

And you said, "You know, my parents are the ones who are paying for us to be here. These rooms are very expensive—"

And he said, "Oh, good, yeah, so I guess everything's settled then. I guess they *didn't* fuck me up when I was a kid because now they're letting me tag along on their expensive vacation."

"I don't know why you're taking it out on me. None of that is my fault!"

"You think I want to get into this shit? I just wanted to go to the beach!"

And you put your hands on your hips and said, "Okay. Let's go to the beach."

And he said, "No, now you're being a brat. Are you on like five different periods right now or what?"

You went to the beach. And Jordan was there, waiting. West got a beer and Jordan got a beer, and every few minutes, they would start giggling for no reason it seemed, and you would say, "What's so funny?"

And West would say, "Nothing. It's stupid."

And Jordan would say, "It's an inside joke."

Then your mother walked by and asked if you wanted to get a massage at the resort spa and you said, "YES."

How was the massage? It was fine, whatever, it was great. Thanks, Mom.

Later, you found West at the poolside bar, talking to the woman who had gotten out of the cab with her husband that first night, the drunk woman who thought it was so funny that there was a dog.

West smiled at you. "Hey, Heather, you remember Amy? This is my kid sister, Heather."

"Aww," Amy said. "Cute."

West winked at you.

And you said, "I have to go."

That night, you all met up for dinner at a hole-in-the-wall restaurant your mother found on the internet. West had a green bruise on his face that looked like the early stages of a black eye. "Oh my God, what happened to your face?" your mother said.

"I got into a fight with a seagull," said West in his signature dry style that made it clear he was joking but unclear what exactly the joke was.

"I don't understand," said your father. "How did you get in a fight with a seagull?"

West shrugged. "We got in a fight. We had a difference of opinion, but it's all settled now."

Dinner was fine; you had a quesadilla. At one point your parents excused themselves and West said, "That's how you know you've been living with someone too long—if you have to go to the bathroom at the same time."

You looked at him. "Did Amy's husband do that to your eye?"

And he said, "Why do you always gotta poke at shit, Heather? Why can't you ever just let shit be shit?"

And you said, "Jesus Christ."

And he said, "All night, you've been looking at me; you know what that feels like?"

And you said, "You're mad at me because I looked at you?"

And he said, "Please don't start. I get enough stupid teenager bullshit from Jordan, believe me. Christ, it's like high school all over again with you two."

And you said, "You're the one who slept with her—no one told you to do that. I don't even know what you see in her, honestly; she's a total ditz and she has wide hips."

West laughed. "God, you two are exactly the same. You act like you're friends, but you say the meanest shit about each other when the other one's not around."

Your face got hot. It hadn't occurred to you that the two of them had talked about you when you weren't there.

"I don't know what you expect from me," he said, and you started, "I expect you—" but he didn't wait for you to finish: "You're just like your mom, you know that? Did you think you were going to come down here and get some real, authentic, genuine experience? What do you think we are? You don't know me. We have these dinners together and everyone acts like we're some kind of family. But we're not a family. We're fucking tourists."

You leaned back in the booth. "You got some food on your face."

He wiped his face with a napkin. "Did I get it?"

"Yeah."

Your parents came back to the table. "Your father and I thought it might be nice to go salsa dancing tonight, all four of us. We found this place in town where they'll teach you."

"I don't think I'm going to do that, June," said West, pushing a piece of meat around his plate with a tortilla chip. "You know, 'cause of my foot and everything."

"Your foot is fine," your father snapped. "Damn it, we paid for you to fly down here to be with the family, not to sit by yourself on the beach getting drunk all day."

West looked up, and for a second it seemed like he might pick up a plate and chuck it at your father's head, but instead he said, "Okay. Let's go salsa dancing."

The salsa dancing was not quite as intimate as you would have liked/disliked. The instructor had you constantly switching partners, so you danced a little with West, a little with your father, and a little with strangers. You danced mostly with strangers.

"That was fun," your mother said, flushed. "I thought that was fun."

As your parents debated how much to tip the instructor, you and West wandered outside to get some fresh air and/or a cigarette. You stood out on the curb in silence for a minute. West coughed and said, "Hey, Heather?"

And you said, "Yeah?"

And he said, "Sometimes I feel like I don't have to tell you things, because I feel like when you look at me, you can see everything."

At the time you didn't say anything, because honestly you didn't have the energy to argue with him anymore, but later you realized this was his best and only attempt at an apology.

So, Saturday.

When you woke up, West was lying in bed, asleep, with his shirt off. This was the first time you'd seen him with his shirt off; his back and arms, as it turned out, were awash in inscrutable tattoos, faded and scarred, another mystery that would never be explained.

After breakfast, your parents went over the bill with the front desk ("My son charged *how* many drinks to the room?"), and West carried your luggage out to the curb. He was leaving on a flight later that afternoon and his plan had been to spend his last few hours on the beach, but now he wasn't so sure. "I'm kind of over the whole resort thing," he said. "Maybe I'll leave my bags here and just dick around town for a little bit."

You thought about your flight home, and you thought about the coming summer. You and Katie Connor had gotten jobs as lifeguards at the city rec center. You were sure she would have a week's worth of gossip to fill you in on, never once asking you about your trip to Puerto Vallarta.

Then you thought about college, what your roommate would be like, what classes you'd take, and all the adventures that lay in front of you, as long and complex as the whole long history of Mexico.

And West said, "Hey, don't be a stranger, okay?" And he looked at you. And he gave you a weak kind of smile and a shrug, as if to say, "Well . . ." And for some reason, that little nothing was enough to set you off. You started crying, right there in front of the hotel, while the bellhops loaded your bags onto the airport shuttle. You started crying, not because of anything West said or did really, just—you started crying.

And West got real uncomfortable and kind of ignored you for a second and looked around like there was maybe someone he might know that you were embarrassing him in front of. And he said, "Hey, come on. You don't need to . . . That's enough." You tried to stop, but that just made you cry more, and he said, "Hey, for real, stop it, would you? You're giving me the creeps. Hey, I'm serious, cut it out. Stop it. Stop it. Please stop it. Please. Please?" This last "please" was too much, and you shook your head and you looked up at him, and he didn't say it, but you could tell he was thinking:

Yeah. I know.

Lunch

with the Person Who Dumped You

You get an email from your ex-whatever-it-was-you-two-were-exactly, asking to meet for lunch. The tone of the email is friendly, casual, if a bit stiff. You agree in a friendly, casual, if a bit stiff email of your own, and a date is set. But what kind of lunch will it be? Hold your breath and SPIN! THAT! WHEEL!

The No-Hard-Feelings Lunch

This is probably the best-case scenario. You can be friends again and put all this ugliness behind you.

"You and me, we're okay, right?"

You'll agree that whatever it was that you had was nice, for what it was, but the timing was bad, you wanted different things, you're two different people, after all; it was "Just One of Those Things," as Ella Fitzgerald sang, but minus the part about it being a trip to the moon on gossamer wings.

You'll offer each other weak declarations that there are no bad guys here (because there aren't, not really) and half-hearted promises that you're not reviled by each other's friends, that there haven't been long, heated conversations about how much you suck. Most important, though, is the unspoken understanding that both of you are people—weak, wounded, fragile, forgivable people doing the very best you can under the impossible circumstance that is day-to-day existence.

In the great grand scheme of things, this is nothing, this wound—it's a nick of a razor, a scrape of the knee—and if you say it enough times and with enough vehemence and smile wider each time you say it, you can even convince yourselves. After all, what were you hoping for, really? What was this ever going to be, realistically? Isn't this the best thing that could have possibly happened, for it to have ended now, before somebody really got hurt?

This is much better. This makes sense.

Everything's fine, you can assure each other and yourselves. Everything will always be fine.

The Loaded-Weapon Lunch

Are you prepared for this? Do you have a list, with bullets, ready to go?

The breakup was abrupt. Maybe you didn't say everything you wanted to say to each other; maybe now, with time, you've started to realize all the ways in which you were wronged. I hope you're crafting the righteous indignation in your head, shaping it, sculpting it. What's the sharpest turn of phrase, the cruelest, fastest way to draw blood?

When the sparring begins, hang back, float like a butterfly, let your opponent use up all the good material, then strike. Remember, the one who laughs last laughs longest, so make sure you laugh last and when you do you laugh heartily but with a detached air of none-of-this-really-matters-I-haven't-been-lying-awake-at-night-staring-at-the-ceiling-regurgitating-all-this-pain coolness. This lunch will decide once and for all who is the winner and who is the loser of this breakup. This is the moment you've been training for, the reckoning where at long last justice will be had. The crowd roars. The judge pounds the gavel. O, Glorious Retribution, how sweet thy taste, how bitter thy sting.

This will not be pleasant, this lunch, and you will both feel terrible afterward—it will not at all provide the closure either of you had hoped for—but if there's a silver lining here (and you're not sure there is one), it's the assurance that what you had, whatever it was, had weight. It made an impact. You can put to rest the fear that you were a blip in this other person's life, a footnote. What you did was important. You hurt somebody, and somebody hurt you.

The Reconciliation Lunch

The Tail-Between-the-Legs Apology Lunch. The Tearful I-Miss-You-I-Made-a-Horrible-Mistake-Can-We-Please-Get-Back-Together Lunch.

It probably isn't this, but you should maybe have a plan just in case.

Because if it is this, if your former lover has indeed decided that the wasteland that was your relationship is more attractive than the wasteland that is being alone, you have a couple options and you should consider them both ahead of time.

Option A is yes, yes, yes. You can attack that yes with desperate vigor, charge blindly, romantically, hysterically into yes. Take a match to your pride and turn back the clock and pretend this breakup never occurred. You were fools, both of you—you were different people then, you were children. You can make it work this time, because now you'll know what it is you could have lost. You're really going to try this time, you swear it, this time you'll do everything not in shades of beige and gray but in bright, bold, brilliant, beautiful COLOR.

But then again, maybe you've done a lot of thinking since your split. Maybe you've seen the foolishness of throwing yourself so recklessly headlong into the fray that is this other person. Maybe this was just the splash of cold water that you needed. I mean, let's be realistic, after all.

This is the question and you should have a plan: Do you welcome back love with open arms, or do you, under the auspices of rational thinking, break this person's heart, like this person broke yours?

You should have a plan, but don't get your hopes up. The lunch probably isn't going to be this. There are a lot of things this lunch can be, but it almost certainly isn't this.

The For-Old-Times'-Sake Lunch

If you meet for lunch near one of your apartments, your meal might be a prelude to one more roll in the hay. You know, for old times' sake. You know, for the sake of the old times. All those old times that would be really disappointed if you didn't fool around again, you owe it to them.

Those times.

Of old.

This isn't a reconciliation, and don't fool yourself into thinking this is closure. It's something in the middle. Is it even something? Perhaps, in the loosest sense of the word "something." It's not quite something but slightly more than nothing, this.

It's like a movie adaptation of your favorite novel, a theme park ride version of your favorite movie. It's a Xerox of a Xerox, a shadow of a ghost.

It's gluten-free pasta, this.

But at least it's pasta.

The Here's-Your-Stuff-Back Lunch

What more is there to say?

The world, it turns out, has continued to exist.

The waters have receded. The fires turned to ash.

You knew this day would come, but you didn't want to believe it.

The scars have healed, the universe has cooled, the porcupine that is your cautious heart has uncurled itself, put away its quills, and continued on in whatever random direction it was headed. And a sweater has been sitting in someone else's closet, a barely there reminder of nothing much really.

You had every intention of being depressed forever, but as it turns out, there's work to be done, meals to eat, movies to see, errands to run. You meant to be in ruins permanently, your misery a monument, a gash across the cold hard earth, but honestly, who has the time for that?

Instead, you survived—apparently, you both did—and things are shockingly okay. But a sweater has been sitting in someone else's closet. A book perhaps, or a knitted winter cap.

The memory of whatever spark you had is rusted, corroded, hardly maintained, and scarcely revisited. This was no great affair, this thing. This was no tragic heartbreak. This was just another thing that happened in a long series of things that happened.

Here's your stuff back. Have a nice life.

rufuS.

"Rufus" is a noise that has many meanings. Sometimes when Man-Monster makes noise like "Rufus," what it means is "Come here." Sometimes "Rufus" means "I am currently petting your head." Sometimes "Rufus" means "I am happy to see you," and sometimes it means "I am very upset." I have discerned many meanings of noise "Rufus." I am very smart.

Occasionally, ManMonster is making noises with other ManMon-ster, and in middle of many annoying nonsense noises, ManMonster will make noise "Rufus," and I will look at ManMonster, like: Why did you make noise "Rufus"? And ManMonster will see me looking and will laugh. I do not know why this delights ManMonster so, but I am happy to delight.

ManMonster makes many noises, and part of my job as Companion to ManMonster is to decipher noises and discern meanings. At first I did not care to discern meanings of ManMonster noises, because why should I bother? I am creature with rich interior life; I should waste time trying to discern meanings of grunts and whines from ManMonster? But now I see that ManMonster is very unable to discern meanings of *my* noises, so if we are to understand each other at all, I am the one who must discern meanings, and since we live in same House, it is better for everyone if *someone* understands *someone*. So, fine. We are companions and I discern meanings.

Here is example: When ManMonster is upset, ManMonster makes noise like "Badog!" This is worst noise ManMonster can make. "Badog!" is for when universe conspires to make life miserable and one is without hope. Many times, ManMonster is very frustrated at situation and makes "Badog" at me, like is my fault universe is unfair. This is very frightening for me to see ManMonster agitated so when I am so small, but I know ManMonster is foolish beast and does not know is not my fault for "Badog."

Sometimes is my fault. Sometimes when ManMonster is away I discover LittleSoft to play with and things get out of hand and somehow situation occurs where LittleSoft is destroyed. This I know will not make ManMonster pleased, so when ManMonster returns to House I run into otherRoom so ManMonster will not know it was I who destroyed LittleSoft. I am in otherRoom minding business when ManMonster walks in frontRoom, makes noise like "Ohno!"

I walk in, very casual, like, What is reason for Ohno? I was in otherRoom, no knowledge why should be Ohno. I feel small bad for deceiving ManMonster but know it is for ManMonster's own good. Already ManMonster is upset because of destroyed LittleSoft. If ManMonster knew LittleSoft was destroyed by me, good friend to ManMonster? That would be a very bad situation.

Still, ManMonster is very upset, makes noise like "Badog!" Makes noise like "Whyudo?" I feel bad that in this situation maybe it really is I who is reason for ManMonster's displeasure. Maybe this time I am Badog. This makes me very very regretful about situation with regards to LittleSoft, because in moment I was not thinking about ManMonster, but as soon as LittleSoft was destroyed I knew Man-Monster would not like.

But then I think about how I fooled ManMonster. ManMonster does not know I am reason for destroyed LittleSoft and this is very good. ManMonster does not know this time I am reason for Badog. ManMonster thinks I am Goodog, and thinking I am Goodog makes ManMonster happy so it is good that I make him think this. Maybe, for making him think this, I am Goodog after all? This is question I often ponder. Is better to be truthful? Or is better to keep up appearance, so that others have good thoughts of you, know they can depend? These questions too big for little creature like me. Maybe no correct answers?

ManMonster and I go on morning and evening constitutionals. This is good—see neighborhood, smell many smells, observe other creatures, make waste—this is important. When younger I would make waste in House, but truth is this is not so pleasant, because then waste sits there with you, in House. Is better to make waste outside of House, and now I know is better. Now I make waste during morning and evening constitutional with ManMonster. Is much better this way.

This is sign of big smartness, that I can learn things. I am very proud of this ability. ManMonster is not so smart, does not learn. ManMonster makes waste in House, in special room for making waste. ManMonster thinks if closes door I do not know he makes waste, but I know. I am very smart.

Sometimes I feel like if I do not make waste I will explode, but I know always there will be time when I can go outside and make waste later, and always this is true. ManMonster does not know to wait to go outside. But is okay. ManMonster does not know things he does not know.

During constitutionals I observe many other creatures, big and small. Some creatures have many smells, very interesting. Other creatures have fewer smells, not so interesting. Either way, observing is much pleasant experience for all creatures. I observe front of creature. Then I observe behind of creature. If creature is small like me, creature can observe my behind simultaneous to me observing creature's behind. Otherwise, we take turns. Sometimes when I am observing, ManMonster pulls on constraint and makes noise like "Okaaaay timetago."

This is very unnecessary and irksome. Perhaps ManMonster thinks I am done observing? If so, is very illogical notion, because if I am done observing, I leave, and there is no reason for pulling on constraint. If there is more to observe, I will continue to observe, and so also here is no reason for pulling on constraint. But ManMonster does not understand this. Sometimes I feel like if I were to be ManMonster and ManMonster were to be creature, I would be very more diligent in regards to trying to understand desires of creature. But also there are some things ManMonster does that I am not so proficient at, like opening doors, so maybe I would not be so good at being ManMonster after all? Perhaps it is better that I am creature and ManMonster is ManMonster.

One time, during nighttime constitutional, I observe faraway creature, very strange experience. This creature has no ManMonster, has no constraint. It is a large creature, brown, and it looks at me from across much area. I look at LargeBrownCreature with big wonder. Where is constraint for LargeBrownCreature? Where is ManMonster for LargeBrownCreature? Does LargeBrownCreature have Companion? Does LargeBrownCreature have House in which for sleeping? Who opens doors for LargeBrownCreature? Who puts food in dish? I wonder if LargeBrownCreature looks at me and thinks me foolish for being constrained by ManMonster. Maybe LargeBrownCreature thinks there is no need for ManMonster. Perhaps LargeBrownCreature thinks I am very much not smart. This angers me, so I make noise at LargeBrownCreature. LargeBrown-

Creature runs off, unconstrained, and ManMonster makes noise like, "Comon Rufus. Lessgo."

Next day, food in dish tastes different to me. Not bad. Just different.

One day, much later, during morning constitutional, I am observing creature—small, like me, with white hair; smells strong, been many places—and I notice this time that ManMonster does not pull on constraint. Instead, ManMonster is making noises with other ManMonster attached to constraint of LittleWhiteHairedCreature. This other ManMonster is tall and skinny and smells of much body movement. Both ManMonsters laugh and make many jovial noises. I look up at ManMonster, like, Okay, I am done observing this creature now and ready to observe other situations. But ManMonster does not pay attention. ManMonster is laughing, making very exuberant noises and sounds at TallSkinny.

Later, TallSkinny appears at House. This is very good because TallSkinny has smells of LittleWhiteHairedCreature, which is very interesting to me. I jump at him and observe all smells. TallSkinny makes noise like, "Oh! Helloggenn!" and ManMonster makes noise like, "Rufus! Dow!" ManMonster and TallSkinny make noises at each other and leave House through door. I try to go with, but ManMonster closes door before I can get out. ManMonster often forgets that I cannot open door, so if he closes door when I am inside then I must stay inside. I try to remind ManMonster I am still inside by making many loud noises, but ManMonster is distracted by TallSkinny and does not come back to let me out of door.

On this night, ManMonster does not return until very late. Is not bad thing ManMonster returns to House so late. Just observation.

Next thing is, TallSkinny appears at House many times. Sometimes TallSkinny appears and then both ManMonsters leave. Sometimes TallSkinny stays and both ManMonsters sit on BigSoft and look at Noisy flatBox and laugh. If there is one thing I have discovered about ManMonsters, it is that ManMonsters love to look at Noisy flatBox and laugh.

Sometimes, TallSkinny comes over with LittleWhiteHairedCreature, and ManMonster makes noise like, "Dubbledate! Dubbledate!" ManMonsters look at Noisy flatBox while LittleWhiteHairedCreature and I run from frontRoom to otherRoom. This is very thoughtful of ManMonster, to spend time with TallSkinny so that I can run from room to room with other creature. It occurs to me: How nice! ManMonster has found a companion for his companion! I know is not always easy for ManMonster, to have so many in House, because sometimes ManMonster becomes very agitated at TallSkinny and much shouting occurs. Other times, they wrestle and nip at each other, and I cannot discern if is playful or if is angry.

On one night, when ManMonster and TallSkinny are looking at Noisy flatBox, LittleWhiteHairedCreature goes into otherRoom and jumps onto otherRoom BigSoft. This is very inappropriate. I know this. I make noise at LittleWhiteHairedCreature to suggest, Hey, maybe you should not be on that? Maybe ManMonsters will not like? I run to frontRoom to alert ManMonster of situation. I make many noises to indicate, There is creature on otherRoom BigSoft! I know creatures should not be on otherRoom BigSoft, only frontRoom BigSoft. But ManMonster is unconcerned. He makes noise like, "Quiii Rufus!" I look at ManMonster. I look at TallSkinny. Both just sit on frontRoom BigSoft and look at Noisy flatBox.

I go back into otherRoom. LittleWhiteHairedCreature is burrowing into BigSoft. I think, Maybe is okay? Maybe this time creatures are allowed on BigSoft? I jump on BigSoft. Is nice. Is soft.

Rufus.

Everywhere is smells of ManMonster. I lie down. Amazing feeling. Feels like I am surrounded always by embrace of ManMonster. Feels like a House inside of House. I have very much joy and I look over at LittleWhiteHairedCreature also on BigSoft and I see DISASTER. LittleWhiteHairedCreature has made waste. On top of BigSoft. This I know is bad news.

Firstly I am paralyzed with fear. What to do? Alert ManMonster or no? I am Companion to ManMonster and I know I should alert of all situations inside of House, but this is news ManMonster will very not like. This is Badog kind of news. It occurs to me, maybe if I don't alert, ManMonster will discover later, will not know who made waste on BigSoft. Maybe ManMonster will think *he* made waste on BigSoft and then forgot? But downside is maybe he will think *I* made waste on BigSoft! This is worst-possible scenario, very much bad to imagine. I realize now I must alert.

I run into frontRoom, make many loud noises.

ManMonster makes noise at me like, "Rufus! No!"

I run back into otherRoom and then back into frontRoom, making noises all the way, as if to say, Come! Look in this room!

ManMonster makes noise like, "Rufus! Quiiiiii!"

TallSkinny makes noise like, "Quiiiii, Rufus!"

Consequently, I am very even more upset, because now Tall-Skinny thinks he can make noise "Rufus" at me? We are not companions. I do not know this other ManMonster.

For review: TallSkinny brings other creature into *my* House. TallSkinny's companion creature makes waste on *my* ManMonster's BigSoft. Now I am trying to alert ManMonster, because I am smart, and now for this I am considered nuisance. I am considered Badog. Is all very very upsetting. I am much alarmed if this is to be state of things. I keep making noise.

ManMonster gets up off of frontRoom BigSoft so that I will know he is serious. He makes noise like, "Rufuuuus . . ."

I run back into otherRoom so that ManMonster will follow me. But instead ManMonster closes door between rooms. This is bad. ManMonster knows I cannot open doors!

At this point in situation, I am much exasperated that ManMonster does not understand me. I work very hard to discern meanings of ManMonster noises but ManMonster makes no effort to discern meanings of my noises! Why should this be? Things would be very easier if I could make noise to ManMonster and ManMonster would think, "Oh, I understand. My companion means to tell me that other creature has made waste on my BigSoft. How wonderful that I have Companion to tell me such things and how wonderful that I can understand!" Instead I make noise, and ManMonster thinks, "I do not understand. I do not like noise. Noise is bad. Surely there is no reason for Companion is making noise. Surely he just makes noise because he does not know I do not like. I must scold him! That is best solution!" Is exhausting.

Later I think back on this and I feel bad. Is not ManMonster's fault he does not understand. ManMonster cannot discern meaning. Only I can discern meaning. I am smart. ManMonster is not so smart. Is not ManMonster's fault.

But now I am trapped in otherRoom with waste of other creature. This is a terrible situation. I make many noises. I scratch at door. LittleWhiteHairedCreature makes noises as well. I am much pleased that LittleWhiteHairedCreature has now decided to contribute, but also I know all this is LittleWhiteHairedCreature's fault in first place, so LittleWhiteHairedCreature is not in clear yet, as far as my book goes.

ManMonster opens door. ManMonster is furious. He grabs con-

Rufus.

straint and pulls hard. He makes noise like, "Rufus! Watt!" Sometimes when he makes noise "Rufus" I know it is good, but this is not
good "Rufus." I am very scared of what ManMonster might do to
me when so angry. But then ManMonster smells, and I see that he
is observing. He goes to BigSoft. He sees waste. Makes noise like,
"Joooooooooooe!"

TallSkinny walks in, observes waste on BigSoft, makes noise like,
"Oh! Hoodiddis?"

ManMonster makes noise like, "NahRufus. IdinkLadybug."

TallSkinny makes noise like, "Ladybug? Joodoo? Oopsie."

Now ManMonster is very upset. "Oopsie? Oopsie?!"

TallSkinny shrugs. "Relaxisaccident! Snahbigdeal. Chillowwww."

And ManMonster makes noise like, "ImnahmaddabouddaLady-
buhh. Buhyucuhbee alilmorsorry."

"Aryuseriosrighnow? Doyuwamme tocleenutup? Aryudatbigababy?"

"Imnotbeanababy towanyuta cleenupaftaryorowndawwg!"

TallSkinny makes very serious demeanor. He makes noise like,
"Whaddis relly bout?"

After this event, TallSkinnyManMonster does not come back to
House so much. LittleWhiteHairedCreature does not come back
to House so much.

In theory, is not so bad. Is more time for me and ManMonster.
More time for long constitutionals. More time for ManMonster to
throw ball for me to retrieve.

But ManMonster does not want to go on long constitutionals.
ManMonster does not want to throw ball for me to retrieve. All
ManMonster wants now is to sit on frontRoom BigSoft and look at
Noisy flatBox.

In past, Noisy flatBox has made ManMonster much jovial, but
now ManMonster is very saddened. At first, I think ManMonster

is still upset about creature making waste on otherRoom BigSoft, but upon continued reflection, this does not speak to true situation. Waste has been removed from otherRoom BigSoft for very long time now, and ManMonster still sleeps on otherRoom BigSoft, so this cannot be concern. Sometimes even ManMonster allows me to sleep on otherRoom BigSoft with ManMonster, which was never allowed before. Very clearly ManMonster is no longer upset about soiled BigSoft. So what is reason for ManMonster to be continued upset? Is mystery.

ManMonster has female ManMonster friend who sometimes comes to House, brings food for ManMonster, takes me on constitutionals. FemaleManMonster is friendly, has many good smells, but is not same as ManMonster.

Sometimes, ManMonster and FemaleManMonster sit for very long time, make many hushed noises. FemaleManMonster makes noise like, "Ushud avvaparty. For yur birdday."

ManMonster shakes head, makes noise like, "Imnah innamood."

FemaleManMonster scratches ManMonster's back, makes noise like, "Uwillbee. Ipromiss."

One night, there is big gathering of ManMonsters. At first, is fun. Everyone wants to pet. I jump up on ManMonsters and they laugh and dance with me. Many delicious foods are dropped on floor and I am able to eat them.

But more and more ManMonsters begin to congregate. Soon, noise becomes unbearable. There is no space to roam—everywhere is foreign ManMonster legs. Strange ManMonsters I do not know pick me up and pull on me. I make noise, like, Put Me Down, but StrangeManMonster does not comprehend. I kick and scratch and StrangeManMonster drops me. I look for main ManMonster, *my* ManMonster, but do not find. I think, Oh, he is gone forever, and get very sad and scared. I look for FemaleManMonster, companion to ManMonster, but do not find. I even look for TallSkinnyManMonster, but do not find. Is this my life now, forever? In crowded House, surrounded by StrangeManMonsters I do not know? I become quite certain that this is my life now, forever.

Now, when I am thinking about this, terrible-on-top-of-terrible thing happens. I make waste in House. This is very unlikely event to occur because I am not one to make waste in House—everyone knows this about me—but is overwhelming, so many ManMonsters. When it is happening I truly do not know it. I look down and see waste and I think, Who made this waste in House? Then I know: I made waste in House.

One of ManMonster's ManMonster friends sees me and shouts many noises. ManMonster runs over: "Ohnononononononowhyyyyyy!!" I am very relieved that ManMonster is not, as it turns out, gone forever, but also at same time I am very ashamed.

ManMonster grabs constraint and pulls me to door. ManMonster opens door and takes me outside like maybe I want to make waste again. I do not. Waste already made. This is very obvious. ManMonster goes back inside. Closes door. I scratch at door, so ManMonster will remember that I cannot open door, so that ManMonster will come back and open door for me, but door does not open.

I look up at sky.

I hear howling of distant creature.

I think about LittleWhiteHairedCreature who made waste in House and then did not come back to House. I think about how after LittleWhiteHairedCreature made waste, TallSkinny did not come back to House. I wonder where they went. Is this where now I must go? I know, if so, is very appropriate. Is what I deserve. Already, ManMonster was very upset. ManMonster did not also need for greatest companion to make waste in House. This is betrayal at worst possible time. Now I truly know what it means to be reason for Badog.

I think about LargeBrownCreature, who had no ManMonster companion and no House. When I saw before, from across much distance, I wondered how it was like to be LargeBrownCreature with no constraint. Now I feel bad to have wondered. Now I know. Is not good. Is not very happy to feel like this.

ManMonster opens door and I am much relieved. He sits down on step next to me. He makes noise like, "Ay-yi-yi . . ." I am very ashamed to have made waste in House—I know when I did this I was not a good companion—but also I do not want to be a creature who is not allowed back in House. I look at him and make face like, Please do not condemn me from House. I can be a very good companion from now on. I will be always good to you from now on. I know ManMonster is not always smart about discerning meaning, but hopefully this time he will discern.

ManMonster scratches my back and he makes noise like, "Rufus rufus rufus." And I know that noise "Rufus" can mean many things. Sometimes "Rufus" means "I am happy to see you" and sometimes it means "I am upset," and this time I discern that it means both things at once. Somehow this time when ManMonster makes noise like "Rufus rufus rufus," it is like all the other Rufuses combined together. It means all the things. It means "Well, here we are." And it means "Yep" and it means "Why?" and "What do we do now?" It means "Goodog" and it means "Badog" and it means "Let me scratch your back for you."

ManMonster makes noise like, "Rufus rufus rufus," and he scratches my back and I love him. I love him with everything I am. I love him like he's a part of myself.

RULES
FOR
TABOO

Draw a card. The word at the top is the word you want your teammate to say. The other words are the TABOO WORDS you cannot use while trying to get your teammate to guess your word. You must make your teammate guess your word, WITHOUT using the taboo words.

FOR EXAMPLE:

If your word is TALL, you CANNOT say SHORT, BIG, HEIGHT, SIZE, or TALES, but you CAN say, "*This* is the smallest drink at Starbucks," or "Your mother, in heels," or "Last night at Kristen's party, you talked with that good-looking law student in the cocktail dress who was so strikingly *this* for over an hour, and when I told you I wanted to go home, you said, 'Just give me twenty more minutes,' and I said, 'I'd really like to leave,' and you said, 'Can you please just be patient?' And I thought that was a real *this kind of* order. A real *this kind of* order indeed, *Steve*."

If your word is BED, you CANNOT say BLANKET, PIL-
LOW, SLEEP, ROOM, or HEAD, but you CAN say, "Our *this* has
blue sheets," or "On Sundays, we strip the *this* and put the blue
sheets in the laundry and replace them with the peach-colored
sheets." You can also say, "Sometimes, Jillian, if I think too much
about us before going to *this*, I have dreams about dragging a car
through a snowstorm. What do you suppose that means, Jillian? I
guess it might mean I shouldn't think so much about us before going
to *this*, but it's difficult when we share a *this*, when you're right there
in the *this* with me but you seem so far away."

If your word is BREAKFAST, you CANNOT say MEAL,
MORNING, PANCAKE, CLUB, or TIFFANY'S, but you CAN say,
"It was over *this* at the Skylight Diner on Thirty-Fourth Street that
you and I decided to move in together. We had taken a crack-of-
dawn train into Penn Station from your parents' house in Ronkon-
koma. You had an omelet, Steve, and I had a bowl of fruit. You said,
'It's stupid that we're paying rent on two different apartments,' and
I smiled and blushed. To us, the future seemed an endless web of
possibilities, like the many-branched line of the Long Island Rail
Road."

If your word is PARK, you can say, "It was in Fort Greene
this where I first realized I loved you, Jillian. It was August, and
we bought a copy of the Sunday paper to read out in the *this*,
and you took a nap under a red oak, and when the shadow moved
and the sun hit your face, you flinched and then smiled. And I realized: That's what I wanted. Just like that. Forever. And it occurred
to me, right there in the *this*, that I had fallen for you completely.
I was irreparably head over heels for this woman who, two months

earlier, had slid up next to me, drunk, at a party and, as if she knew me, slurred into my ear, 'You deserve someone who will love you in all your damaged glory.' "

If your word is CHANGE, you can say, "*This* is what I did, gradually, imperceptibly. I can't say how exactly, but I'm not the same person you fell in love with in Fort Greene Park that Sunday in August. It's an old cliché that women break up with men because they think they'll *this* and they don't, and men break up with women because they think they won't *this* and they do, but is there also a cliché about why men and women stay together?" You can say that, sure, but why would you want to? You may be better off passing. You can say, "PASS," and your teammate can groan, and you can say, "I'm sorry, Steve, I don't want to do that one." And "Besides," you can say, "this game is stupid. I hate this stupid game. Next time we're playing Jenga."

If your word is TOMORROW, you CANNOT say DAY, TODAY, YESTERDAY, AFTER, or FUTURE—there are a whole lot of things you can't say—but you CAN say, "*This* terrifies me and I don't know why. Maybe I'm just weak. Maybe we're both so incredibly weak."

If your word is EYES, you CANNOT say FACE, NOSE, GLASSES, SEE, or SOUL, but you CAN say, "Last night I looked into your *these* and I hit a wall. I could make out nothing past the iris, and I realized that the deep unquenchable yearning I long thought I had recognized was actually my own. How foolish of me. How foolish of us all."

You can pass, and then your teammate can pass, and then you can thank your guests for coming, and for the cheesecake they brought, and as you clear the wineglasses from the living room, you can say, "This was fun," in an absent tone that makes it clear that you don't really mean it, but you don't exactly *not* mean it either. And before you crawl off to your blue-sheeted bed, you can pack up the game and put it back on a shelf in the living room closet, where you don't have to look at it until you drag it out for the next party, where you don't even have to think about it.

up-and-comers

"Do you ever think maybe you're overthinking things?" Lizzy asked.

We were getting breakfast together, as we often did, the morning after a very long night, as we'd often had. She was nursing a black eye, as she often was, and we were both nursing hangovers, as we almost always were, and we were talking about a boy who'd asked me out on a date and we were weighing the pros and cons of me going out with him.

"I *do* think I'm overthinking things," I said. "I think that all the time. But then I think, What if I'm *not* overthinking things? What if I'm just regular-thinking things but then I *think* I'm overthinking things because I subconsciously want to let myself off the hook?"

Lizzy stirred the vodka into her coffee. "You might be overthinking things."

I shrugged a *yeah, well . . .* shrug and said, "Yeah, well . . ."

"You know what I think, Porkchop?" Lizzy had started calling me "Porkchop" recently as a reference to an inside joke I was now too embarrassed to admit I didn't remember. "I think you're afraid of putting yourself out there because you're afraid of getting hurt, because you are—and I believe this is the clinical term—a fucking coward."

"Okay, well, first of all, I am not a coward. I actually saved the world from subterranean bioterrorists just this week."

Lizzy scrunched up her face in her trademark Lizzy who-gives-a-shit scowl. "Yeah, but that's like a Tuesday for you. You have super-strength and photon blasts. I mean, don't get me wrong, it's awesome that you did that, but when's the last time you did something that actually scared you?"

This is a story about superheroes, kind of. I mean, I guess that's the stuff that everyone wants to hear about—the crazy powers and colorful villains and us all working together to vanquish evil and all that—but actually this is a story about a rock band. Before everything went to shit, Clay used to say he never asked to be a superhero; he just wanted to be a rock star. Well, that's true of me too, I guess, except I didn't even really want to be a rock star. I just wanted to get drunk.

I was twenty-three years old and I was living in the Mission and I was scraping by with a hostess job at a restaurant that specialized in olive-based dishes and I had a couple summer dresses that I didn't look *completely* terrible in, and everything was going fine, like depressingly so, like things were so *fine* I wanted to kill myself. I had somehow fallen into the habit of playing piano for this five-piece alt-folk/fuzz-punk/shoe-core collective called the Up-and-Comers, and I guess we were starting to get pretty good, as far as getting a lot of "likes" on Instagram and people paying attention to us and writing nice things about us in indie music blogs and *SF Weekly* and things like that, and we were talking about going on tour.

Clay (drums, cowbell) had some friends up in Portland and he thought they could get us a gig there and then we could do like a whole Pacific Northwest thing. I had never been to Portland, and I had saved up some vacation days at Why Not Take Olive Me, and things had just kind of fizzled out with this girl I'd been seeing (the less said about her, the better), so I was all for the idea, even though privately I often wondered if maybe the Up-and-Comers weren't actually all that good, as far as, you know, actually being any good.

"I'm so over the whole touring thing," said Joelle (lead vox, strong opinions). "I did it with my last band. You spend a lot of money on gas and you play a lot of empty bars and then you come home and no one remembers you. We should focus on building our fan base in the Bay Area, while we've got some momentum. Besides," she added, "Oregon sucks."

So we didn't go to Portland.

Instead we stayed in San Francisco and opened for Fuck Shit Piss Karate at Brick & Mortar Music Hall, *again,* and I tried to figure out what I really wanted to be doing with my life because I was pretty sure it wasn't this. For some reason I had this idea that I was really special and that I was put here to do something really great and important, but the longer I kept living the more it just seemed like nope, I'm just kind of a normal person just like everybody else.

That's when Mutt Wang told us about this Battle of the Bands he'd heard about up near Tahoe. Mutt was a guy Lizzy knew from college; he called himself our "manager," but mostly what that meant was that he would wear a tie to our gigs and buy us all drinks.

We had kind of a regular audience at this point—including Lizzy's girlfriend, Kathleen, Iris's weird uncle who always wore a captain's hat and asked us to call him the Mariner (welcome to San Francisco), and like half a dozen guys who all thought they were Joelle's boyfriend—but sometimes we'd play shows and Mutt would be the only person there, sitting by himself in a booth in the back and smiling dumbly when we played "Not Hardly" as if he'd never heard it before. The most striking thing about the guy was how *decent* he was, like how he'd always be the first person to ask if you were cold and do you want to wear his coat, and also could he buy you a drink.

"You should really do this Battle of the Bands," Mutt said. "I think we need to start thinking bigger than just the Bay Area."

"Oh, do *we*?" Joelle said. She was pretty reluctant about the whole thing, as you could probably imagine, but Iris (lead guitar, voice of reason) had this family cabin that we could all stay at up by the lake, a couple miles from the old abandoned government testing facility, and it kind of seemed like a fun excuse to get out of the city.

We piled into Clay's van (all of us except for Mutt, who—he made sure we knew—*wanted* to come, but had a work thing he couldn't get out of, which was totally fine by us, because—Joelle made sure he knew—Mutt *wasn't in the band*). We got to the cabin pretty late and immediately started drinking out by the fire pit.

After a couple beers, I noticed Lizzy had wandered into the house. I found her in the kitchen, leaning against the counter and peeling the label off her beer bottle.

"What's going on? Every time you drink you get all weird and sullen," I said. "Don't be weird and sullen, Lizzy."

She shook her head and tried not to look at me. She scrunched up her face and waved me off, the futile kind of I-don't-want-to-bother-you-with-my-troubles gesture you make at a good friend who you know wants nothing more than to be bothered with your troubles.

"Lizzy, what is it?"

"Kathleen and I broke up."

"Oh my God, are you okay?"

"I'm fine," she said, unfinely. She pulled another beer from the fridge.

"What happened?"

"I don't know. I just keep thinking, it's not supposed to be this hard, you know? But I always make it hard. But then again, maybe it's her fault, because she broke the first rule of rock and roll."

"What's that?"

I watched her fumble with the latch on the screen door, and as she pushed out into the night she shouted back at me, "Never fall in love with the bass player!"

I followed her back to the fire. Joelle raised an eyebrow. "Where were you two?"

"Yeah," said Clay. He had taken Iris's acoustic guitar and he started half singing to himself as he strummed. "Wheeeere were youuuuuuu twoooooo?"

"We were just talking," I said.

"Well, I'm glad you're back," said Iris, "because I actually have something I want to give you all." She grabbed her backpack and pulled out these hemp necklaces she'd made for all of us, each with a single blue bead she'd gotten from the strange mystic who lived in the apartment below her and was always stinking up the place with weird incense and taxidermied roadkill (welcome to San Francisco).

Well, we all put the necklaces on, but this started a whole conversation, once again, about What Kind of Band We Were. At this point we were really getting pretty expert at starting conversations about What Kind of Band We Were and could probably get it going from just about anything.

"So, that's what we are now? A band that wears matching necklaces?"

"Come on, Joelle."

"What, no one else thinks that's super-corny?"

Still noodling on the guitar, Clay sang, "Oh, I-I-I-I-I-I-I-I-I-I-I don't even know why we're having this conversation about necklaces when meanwhile we're still playing songs we wrote three years ago."

"Bands play old songs, Clay. Bands do do that."

"Okay, but everyone just heard Iris say doo doo, right?"

"Yeah, but I don't want to just be *a* band, you know? Like don't you guys ever dream of something mo—"

Suddenly a bolt of lightning shot down from the clear black sky, hitting Lizzy's necklace and ricocheting off our five blue beads, knocking us back into the woods, scattering us into the dead leaves like eraser shavings across a page.

"Is everyone okay?" I shouted.

"Okay-ish," said Iris, stumbling as soon as she stood up. She rested a hand on a rock, and the whole ground kind of shook and then like ten feet away a little tree fell over.

"Emphasis on the *ish*," said Joelle. She was floating three feet in the air. Her eyes looked like they were on fire.

So, I don't know if it was the lightning, or the mystic's beads, or our proximity to the old abandoned government testing facility, or the fact that we were all drunk, or if this is just a thing that happens sometimes, but we all got superpowers that night. Again, I really don't want to harp on the superpowers part of it all—I'd hate to think that the fact that I could now shoot photon blasts out of my fists was like the most interesting thing about me, as opposed to, I don't know, my sparkling personality—but there were two basic rules to the superpowers: 1) we had to wear our necklaces with the blue beads in order for our powers to work, and 2) we had to be drunk. And the drunker we got, the more powerful we became.

When we got back down to the city, there was some talk about maybe starting up some sort of superhero team, but honestly, it all kind of seemed like a lot of to-do.

"I just feel like the whole using-our-powers-for-good thing is kind of a cliché at this point," said Joelle (lead vox, fire-laser eyes, flight). "Like what are we supposed to do, just wander the streets, waiting until we see someone get mugged? It doesn't seem like the best use of our time."

But then Iris (lead guitar, kinetic vibration, teleportation) gave this really stirring speech about like responsibility and all that, and what it means to be a citizen of this universe, and the social contract or whatever. I wish I could remember it better, because it sounds super-hokey when I paraphrase it, but it really was a pretty great speech, super-inspiring, and it totally made you feel like everything happened for a reason and there was a noble thread sewn into the tapestry of your narrative and, just by existing in this world, you were a part of something wonderful. But I don't know; maybe you kind of had to be there.

So then we were superheroes for a while, and that was a whole thing.

I don't remember all of it, the superhero stuff, because it was kind of a *lot* and I was fantastically drunk during most of the important parts, but it comes back in sparks and flashes, those nights. It was broken-bottle-in-the-street nights, busted-nose-from-a-fifty-foot-fall kind of three-day weekends. It was nights of stumbling, falling, laughing, shouting, punching, crawling, screaming, crying, leaping, flying, living, drinking, singing, drinking—we wrestled angels, real honest-to-God fallen angels all fucked up on amphetamines, and we battled sea creatures as tall as the Transamerica Pyramid, and stayed up all night shooting the shit about fucking nothing, and fucked groupies, and stopped bank robberies, and did interviews where reporters would ask questions like, "Is it true you're impenetrable?" and Joelle would get real close to the tape recorder and, without breaking eye contact with the interviewer, say, "I can't speak for the others, but I've been penetrated hundreds of times."

We'd get mobbed by the press, microphones shoved in our faces, flashbulbs exploding, stopped in the street on our way to save the world. "How do you stay humble?" And wiping the whiskey off our lips, we'd stumble-leap into flight or something like it toward whatever next adventure and shout back behind us, "We don't."

Joelle's harem of admirers went from a half dozen to a couple hundred seemingly overnight. Pretty girls would spill up to Clay in bars and diners and say, "Hey, aren't you one of the Up-and-Comers?" and Clay (drums, cowbell, molecular absorption of the kinetic energy and physical density of objects) would smirk and say something super-cheesy like, "Well, I'm up but I'm not coming."

But Lizzy was the worst. She'd go right up to them, these women, sitting alone or with friends, or with their girlfriends or even boyfriends, husbands, it didn't matter. She'd go up and say, "Hey, what are you doing with this guy? Here's the deal: I'm hella good in bed, I play bass guitar, and I have the power of spooky hexagons. You want to get out of here?"

Meanwhile, there was always a villain to battle, a lawsuit to settle, a licensing agreement to negotiate. Mutt Wang quit his job and started working for us full-time as our business manager. I don't know what we would have done without Mutt, really I don't. Like, how are superheroes supposed to stay in the black? Especially superheroes who are drunk all the time and constantly knocking over buildings. Mutt rented a space for us downtown that we could use as our base of operations, and in her spare time, Iris converted it into an interdimensional helisphere.

So, you know when your favorite band signs on to a major label, and it's exciting and you're happy for them, but then their new album comes out and it sounds overproduced and super-poppy and you sort of forget what made them special in the first place? Well, I hate to say it, because it's such a cliché at this point, but that's kind of what happened to us with the introduction of the interdimensional helisphere.

Suddenly we were traveling to distant moons and hypothetical worlds and battling even worse guys with worms for heads and arms for legs in dimensions within dimensions, but even with all the craziness going on around us we tried to keep our feet on the ground (or, if not the ground, then at least on one of Lizzy's spooky hexagons) and remember who we were.

One time, Clay, so drunk he could barely stand, beaten to an inch of his life by Dorjak the Destroyer, vomited onto the ragged plains of Earth-12 an entire pitcher of raspberry mojito and, while absorbing the kinetic energy of the fossilized ancient heart of an alien warrior king, turned to me, smiled dumbly, and asked, "Hey, who do you think will be the first one of us to get married?"

Turned out it was Joelle, breaking a couple thousand hearts with the wedding announcement: "I Only Have Fire-Laser Eyes for You." She had a pretty sweet wedding too, except for the part where the DJ wouldn't play "Cotton-Eyed Joe," no matter how many times Lizzy and I requested it, and also the part where the Shadowman attacked us right in the middle of the cake cutting, which, if you ask me, was a super-dick move. Well, we all got wasted real fast and defeated the Shadowman and his lemming army, *again,* but the wedding was more or less ruined and Joelle's husband, Sam, was really upset.

"I just wanted one day that wasn't about you and your superhero friends—*one day* that was about us."

What I mostly remember from that time are the talks. Long conversations with Iris about Truth and Justice and Society, and bitch sessions with Joelle about which supervillains were actually kind of cute and which ones were total dicks, and lazy rambling pow-wows with Lizzy, holed up in diners and bars until three, four, five, six, seven, eight, nine in the morning, frothy mixes of inside jokes and bittersweet reveries over exes and philosophical quandaries and mumbled ponderings over what does it take to get some goddamned service in this place.

Lizzy was the first person I told when Mutt Wang asked me out.

"*Mutt* Mutt? *My* Mutt?" Lizzy cackled out a mouthful of corn-flakes. "What did you tell him?"

I shrugged. "I said I'd think about it."

Lizzy nodded thoughtfully. "You should hella go out with him, Porkchop. You could use a stabilizing force in your life."

"Oh, *I* need a stabilizing force? Should we drill down into *your* love life?"

"That hardly seems relevant."

"Are you finding deep emotional fulfillment in the parade of bimbos you take home?"

"They're not bimbos."

"I'm sorry, the parade of scintillating conversationalists, the paragons of wit and class . . ."

Lizzy crossed her arms. "There is nothing less attractive in a woman than a hatred of other women."

I rolled my eyes and performed the international symbol for jerking off. "I'm devastated you don't find me attractive. Truly. It keeps me up at night."

Lizzy smiled. "For real, though, you should go out with Mutt. You like Mutt."

"You don't know who I like."

"I know everything about you. Besides, when was the last time you dated a guy? If you don't do *something* with a penis in the next"—she looked at her watch—"week and a half, I think they're going to take away your bi card."

I laughed. "Is that how it works? Because that is super cisnormative."

"Don't change the subject."

"What subject?!"

She leaned in. "I think you might be a full-blown lesbian, Porkchop."

"And what are you, the welcoming committee?"

"Are you kidding? I already have to compete with Iris. I'm trying to get you off the market here."

"Oh, now I see what this is about."

"I am one hundred percent looking out for my interests, was that not clear?"

"Okay, but what if Mutt and I go out and it's weird and then he's still our manager so I have to see him all the time? Or what if it's not weird—what if it's great—but then *later* it's weird?"

Lizzy grabbed the flask out of my purse and poured some vodka into her coffee. "Do you ever think maybe you're overthinking things?"

So, I went out with Mutt. He took me to this super-shmancy place up in Marin. I told him about how I was trying to teach myself guitar, and he asked if he could come back to my apartment and hear me play something, which I thought was a pretty bold move. I had intentionally not cleaned my apartment before the date, the thinking being that if my apartment was messy I wouldn't bring Mutt home, a kind of advanced not-shaving-my-legs technique, but then I brought him home anyway, so, shows what I know.

I had written this dopey love song for no one in particular, but it didn't really feel ready to play for anyone, and besides, it felt like if I played it for Mutt, then I would really be *saying* something, and I didn't think I wanted to do that. Instead I played a Fleetwood Mac song. I think I did a pretty crummy job of it—I must have missed like half a dozen chords, but Mutt didn't seem to notice, or he pretended not to notice, which I thought was pretty annoying either way, because if he really couldn't tell, did we really want this guy to be our manager, and if he was just pretending I did a good job in order to be nice to me, then that was pretty condescending. But then anyway, Mutt and I had sex.

The next morning, Lizzy immediately cornered me in the helisphere kitchenette.

"How was the sex?" she asked.

I choked on my yogurt. "Did Mutt tell you we had sex?"

"No. You did."

I rolled my eyes. "If you could interrogate evil henchmen half as well as you interrogate me . . ."

Lizzy smiled at me. "Congratulations, Porkchop. Your chops have been thoroughly porked. I'm proud of you."

I did my best impression of Lizzy's trademark who-gives-a-shit scowl. "So, what about you? Are you going to find someone?"

"I find people all the time."

"Yeah, but that's just because you don't care about any of them. I'd like to see you around a girl you actually liked. I bet you'd be the biggest fucking moron in the world."

She didn't say anything. She just looked at me and sipped her coffee.

So, then I was twenty-four for a year, and that was a whole thing.

It was fun, for a little bit, being twenty-four, in that way that all things are fun for a little bit, but at a certain point, it started to dawn on me that as time passed, we were playing music less and less, and blacking out more and more, and it seemed like the longer we'd been doing this, the more alcohol it took to get our powers going, and every time we defeated *this* deposed alien viceroy or *that* disgruntled mutant dolphin, there'd be some other thing just waiting to take its shot at us, and it started to feel like, is this really why any of us got into this in the first place?

One time, Clay asked me if I'd ever thought about quitting. "I mean, we're in our midtwenties. Doesn't that feel kind of too old already to still be fucking around, getting drunk every day and battling psycho lizard-beasts? Like, are we still going to be doing this when we're forty?"

I had to admit he had a point, but frankly, I wasn't really good at anything else.

"Besides," he said lightly, "there are only so many times you can beat up a guy before it starts to mess you up in the head." He chuck-led to himself—awkwardly, sadly.

"Clay," I said. "Those guys we beat up—those are bad guys."

And he said, "I know . . ." And he fiddled self-consciously with the bead on his necklace.

But whenever I would talk to Mutt, who was, I guess, my boy-friend now, about cutting back on the whole superhero thing, he would get really passionate about how this was my calling or what-ever and so few get the opportunity to do what I did and I would be crazy to walk away from all that. "And besides," he would say, "what am *I* supposed to do if you guys all suddenly stopped being superheroes?"

And I don't know if I was ever convinced, not a hundred percent, but I knew that he really cared and I guess I figured that sometimes being in a relationship meant doing things you weren't totally on board with for the sake of making the other person happy.

"Also," he would say, "I need you to sign these forms. This is a standard licensing agreement."

And I loved Mutt, in that way that you love something when you're at a place in your life when you're ready to love something and there's a thing there that you can love. And I still had that dumb little love song I wrote that I was teaching myself how to play on the guitar that I performed for no one. Sometimes I would practice it while Mutt was in the shower and he'd come out and say, "What were you singing just now?" and I'd say, "Nothing," and it felt good to have a thing that was mine and mine alone.

And I enjoyed being in the band, and I did think what we were doing was important, but more and more often, someone would get sloppy with the math and land on the wrong side of plastered. We'd be fighting the Osmonaut, and in the midst of battle, Clay would just start checking his phone for text messages, and it was like, hey, can we focus here?

Some nights, instead of going home, Joelle would drink herself to sleep on the couch at the helisphere, and the next morning, when one of us would ask her if everything was okay with her and Sam, she'd say, "I'm fine, it's just—I spend so much time here anyway, and Sam and I live all the way in Berkeley and it's such a hassle trying to get over the bridge," which kind of made sense, but also on the other hand, Joelle could fly, so I didn't really get why rush-hour traffic would be a going concern for her.

And then there was the time Lizzy and I were holed up in an air duct in the CyberCorp building, trying to figure out how to bring down the Mad Goddess Suspira, who had just assembled all the Proto-Universe Crystals into an unstoppable Power Scepter, when Lizzy suddenly got all sullen and antisocial and just looked at her feet and mumbled, "What's the point? I mean, what's even the point of anything?"

And I said, "Lizzy, this is not the time for this. Did you drink red wine? You can't do that; you get all sad and sleepy."

"I saw Kathleen," she slurred. "Did I tell you? I saw Kathleen?"

I shook my head.

"I've been trying to get in touch with her, and for a while, she was just ignoring me. But then after I saved that little girl from the sentient BART train last week, finally Kathleen agreed to meet up."

"Lizzy, that's huge." Through the slats of the air duct I could see Suspira loading her Power Scepter into CyberCorp's Time Vibration Laser.

"So I saw her last night. And I told her, you know, 'Kathleen, I'm still in love with you.' I didn't mean to say it, I wasn't planning on saying it, but it just . . ."

She was getting really worked up and I motioned at her to lower her voice.

She did not lower her voice. "I said, 'I know I wasn't always there for you, but things were so crazy then, and I did a lot of work,' you know, 'I'm not that girl anymore.' But she was just like, 'You *are* that girl, that's the whole point. That's who you are, Lizzy.'"

The whole building started shaking as the Time Vibration Laser powered on.

I said, "Hey, you think we could maybe talk about this later? I'm totally invested in this story and I definitely want to hear about it, but, you know, the laser and everything . . ."

"And you want to know the worst part?"

The crystals on Suspira's scepter started lighting up, one by one, and Lizzy leaned in close and whispered through a cloud of Merlot breath, "The worst part is she's right."

"Jesus Christ, Lizzy. I get that you're sad, but I can't be your fucking babysitter right now. There are bigger things to deal with. If we don't stop the Time Vibration Laser, it could destroy the planet."

"Psh. You mean the planet where *Kathleen* lives? Kathleen's precious planet?"

I rolled my eyes. "This is not a good color on you."

She shrugged. "What do you want from me? I'm no hero. I'm just Lizzy."

"Yeah, okay. You're Lizzy. And I think you're fucking awesome. I, for one, adore Lizzy, she's the bee's fucking knees. But if you don't get it together and help me stop the Mad Goddess Suspira from firing her crystal-powered laser, then that means Kathleen was right about you."

"Whaaaaaaaaa? No."

"Don't you get it? If all of humanity is destroyed in a fiery time-holocaust that you couldn't stop—*Kathleen wins!*"

"That's fucked-up!" Lizzy exploded out of the air duct and in one swift move cut off the energy of the Power Scepter and pinned Suspira against the wall with some spooky hexagons.

Later, back on the ground, when Iris was explaining to the press what had happened exactly, Lizzy had sobered up a little and she gave me a bashful kind of shrug, like she was saying *Thanks* and *Sorry* and *Thanks again* all at once, and I shook my head at her, like, *Of course.*

Mutt climbed through the crowd of bystanders and grabbed my arm. "Thank God you're okay." He wrapped his arms around me and kissed me, like people do in the movies. I was a little self-conscious, kissing Mutt like that in front of the cameras and everybody, but Mutt said it was good to show everybody that we had personal lives. It humanized us, Mutt said.

We were all pretty jazzed up after that battle, but when we got back to the helisphere, Joelle's husband was waiting for us.

"Sam!" Joelle said in that way you say someone's name that you haven't said in a while.

And Sam shook his head. "No. Don't come near me. It is not okay. You get drunk with your friends, and then you come home . . ."

Joelle looked at the rest of us. "Guys, do you think maybe we could have a minute?"

"Nobody leave," Sam said. "I don't want to be alone with you ever again. Not after what you did."

"What I *did*? Sam . . ."

"You know what you did. Or is *forgetting* another one of your superpowers?"

"I swear I don't know what you're talking about."

"Do you want me to say it? Don't make me say it."

". . . Can we talk about this?"

"Do you want me to say what you did, in front of all your friends? I probably should. I probably should go straight to the media, tell the whole world. Is that what you want? You really want me to say what you did?"

Joelle swallowed hard. "No. I—I know it. I know what I did."

Sam's face fell, as if hearing Joelle admit the thing out loud suddenly made it a different kind of true.

Then Joelle started to say something, but Sam cut her off. "I want you to stay away from me. Do you understand? You need to stay as far away from me as you can get. Don't call me. Don't call my friends. Do you understand? This? Is over."

He took off his wedding ring. He was shaking.

"Sam . . ."

"Tell me you understand."

"I . . . understand."

"Then there is nothing else to say."

And he left. There was a long pause, before Clay said, "Aaaawwk-waaaaard," and we all kind of said, "Shut up, Clay."

We watched Joelle stumble toward the kitchenette, grab a handle of gin out from under the sink and start chugging it.

"Joelle, is that really a good—"

"Not now, Iris. I can't take another one of your fucking speeches right now. I just need . . . I need to get away for a little while, get some air." She weaved toward the window.

"Joelle, I really don't think you should be alone right now."

"No, I just need some air, that's all. I need some air."

And we all watched her drop out the window and then a second later shoot straight up past it into the sky.

Iris grabbed a gin of her own from behind a couch cushion, but

Lizzy said, "Let her go. She just needs to blow off some steam. I'm sure she'll be fine."

And I said, "Yeah. She'll be fine."

Well, she died.

There were conflicting reports about what happened, exactly. She went on a tear through all the bars in Berkeley, and after she died a thousand drunkards came out of the woodwork claiming to be the last person who saw Joelle alive. Some said she was depressed, rambling; others that she was jubilant, euphoric, buying shots for the whole bar, tossing bottles into the air and blasting them with her fire-laser eyes. We do know how she spent her last moments, though; the autopsy confirmed it: she flew straight up into the night sky, as far as she could go, as far away from everything as she could get, and then when the air got too thin to breathe she passed out and gravity dragged her tumbling back down to Earth.

You'd think that might have been some kind of come-to-Jesus moment for the rest of us, Joelle dying, but we were all drinking at her funeral, passing miniature bottles of schnapps behind the pews.

So now the Parents' Council for Appropriate Responsible Behavior or Whatever was suddenly up our butts, because like we weren't good role models for kids because we were drinking all the time, but it was just like, dude, we're not trying to be good role models, we're just trying to keep the streets safe. And my parents were calling every week, like, "Are you as drunk as they say you are on the news?" And I always had to convince them, "No, Mom, you know they just make stuff up to get a good story."

And meanwhile there were all these new superheroes getting all the good write-ups, like A-Man and the Silver Bullets and Captain Boo from the Planet Goo—younger guys who would do even crazier shit than we did—and I guess people started to think of the Up-and-Comers as being kind of old hat. Mutt and I were in bed, watching some dumb late-night show ("Don't you think it's about time they changed their name to the Down-and-Outers?"), when Mutt said, "We need to shift the narrative here. Give the press something positive they can focus on."

"Like what?"

"What if we got married?"

We were a mile above Chinatown, fighting the mayor's evil android hordes, when I casually brought up that Mutt had asked me to marry him. Everybody was really happy for me, except for Lizzy.

"No. You can't marry Mutt. That's crazy."

"Stranger things have happened," I said, as I tore the metallic heart out of a nearby flying goon with my mystical-bead-based superstrength. "Besides, you're the one who told me to go out with him in the first place."

"Yeah, but you can't marry him. I mean, Mutt's a great guy, but he's not the guy you marry."

And Clay said, "Hey, do you guys think the mayor's really gone evil this time, or is this just another one of his clones?"

But Lizzy, all high and mighty on her spooky hexagons, would not be distracted. "You don't love him, Porkchop. I'm telling you, this isn't what you want."

"What is your deal? Why can't you ever just be happy for me?" I asked while I held one of the androids in a headlock and kicked another one in the face. "Why do you always have to know, like, a better way for me to live my life?"

And Iris said, "Guys, can we focus?"

And Lizzy said, "Porkchop, I'm just trying to—"

"I don't know why you fucking call me Porkchop all the time. It's not my name, and it isn't cute."

Lizzy stopped shooting spooky hexagons at the androids for a moment and looked at me. "Okay, I'm sorry." But it wasn't an I'm-sorry "I'm sorry," it was an I-can't-believe-you're-making-me-say-sorry "I'm sorry."

"No," I said. *"I'm* sorry. I'm sorry you can't figure out your own life so you constantly try to control mine."

"What the fuck? I'm not trying to control anything! I'm just trying to be a good friend, you dumb asshole, because I think the fucking world of you and I want you to be happy."

And I said, "Well, great, thank you for your friendship, you've always been a wonderful pillar of support."

And then the last of the androids said, "PREPARE FOR DOOM!" before Iris blew it to pieces by teleporting inside of it.

We dropped down onto the street and waved to the applauding tourists and Chinese shopkeepers, and Lizzy muttered to me, "You know, it actually makes a lot of sense that you'd marry Mutt. Of course you're going to marry him, because that's what Mutt wants and you would never in your life make a decision for yourself."

"You are way out of line."

"Are you just going to keep on stumbling down the path of least resistance all your life? Is that your plan? Jesus Christ, you've become a total fucking bore."

I shot a photon blast at her, which knocked her back into a fish stand.

She got up and rolled her eyes. "Oh, real mature."

"You're real mature," I said.

"Fine!" she said. "Enjoy your fucking married life with your fucking husband and your fucking house in the fucking suburbs with your fucking white fucking picket fucking fence fucking fucking."

She threw her arms up and started walking away, and I shouted at her, "Hey! Excuse me for trying to actually build a life for myself instead of just using this whole superhero thing as an excuse to get drunk and pick up groupies like a fucking bass guitarist cliché!"

She turned around and shot a spooky hexagon at me and then I shot a photon blast at her, and there we were in the middle of China-town shooting photon blasts and spooky hexagons at each other. And then we were wrestling, grabbing at each other's throats, throwing each other down Stockton, tearing across the shops and restaurants, through a mess of cheap fans and plastic shoes and Chinese yo-yos. Clay and Iris had to physically separate us, we were so mad.

On the limo ride to city hall, where we were to be rewarded with another round of medals for our valor, I muttered under my breath, "Look, don't take it out on me just because you're still in love with some chick who will never love you back."

Lizzy shook her head. "Jesus Christ," she said. "You really don't know me at all."

Then Lizzy and I didn't talk, for like a long time. Like we'd still be civil with each other at press events, or like when we had to work together to save the president's daughter or whatever, but we didn't *talk* talk.

So that was a whole thing.

One day we were all not talking to each other in the helisphere kitchenette when Mutt practically dragged Clay in by the ear.

"Tell 'em," said Mutt. "Tell everyone what you did."

Clay rolled his eyes.

"Oh boy," said Iris. "What'd you do this time?"

"Look, sometimes I get aggressive, okay? Like, first of all, can I just say, it's not normal, what we do—what we're *expected* to do—"

"Are you going to tell them, or should I?"

"I'm getting to it, Jesus. So, I've spent the last couple years getting myself into this mind-set, you know, pumping myself up, absorbing all this kinetic energy, so I can do what *everybody wants me* to do . . . and I have this . . . aggression."

"There's a video on the internet," said Mutt, "of Clay absorbing a rum bottle and then smashing his glass fist over a guy's head for cutting him in line at the grocery store."

"Jesus, Clay!"

"What? Who's to say he wasn't being controlled by the Phantom Ventriloquist? I mean, we don't know, right?"

"You can't just go around—" I started to say, but then Mutt cut me off.

"It's a Bacardi bottle."

"And . . . ?"

"Clay absorbed a bottle of Bacardi. We have an exclusive endorsement deal with Captain Morgan; do any of you read the contracts you sign?"

Clay waved him off. "It's really not a big deal."

"It is a big deal. It's their biggest competitor, and the video is everywhere. What were you thinking?"

Lizzy raised a finger. "Uh, is anyone else more concerned about what Clay did to the guy at the grocery store than what it's going to do to our Captain Morgan deal?"

"It's not just Captain Morgan," Mutt sputtered. "You are paid to be brand ambassadors; that is the *source* of our income. If brands can't trust you to do that—I mean, this is the *reason* you exist."

Normally this would be the point of the conversation when Iris would say something really smart and make us all realize the right thing to do, but instead she wandered over to the corner of the room where we kept a set of instruments, picked up her guitar, and started strumming.

She was playing "Not Hardly." Lizzy picked up her guitar and started playing too. Then Clay got behind the drums and I sat at the piano and the Up-and-Comers were playing together for the first time in what must have been forever. It felt a little eerie playing the song without Joelle there to sing it, especially when Iris and Lizzy jumped in and shouted their backup parts on the chorus, the Oh-I-Dos and Yes-It's-Trues, but still, there was something incredibly powerful about everyone just shutting up for a second and playing a song together.

After we finished, we all just stood there in silence, and then Iris said, very simply, "Yeah, I'm gonna go."

"What do you mean go? Go where?"

Iris put down her guitar and put her hands on her hips, indicating she was prepping her body for teleportation. "The iniquity of our world is too systemic to be ameliorated by tackling only the most flagrant of abuses," she declared. She always loved using big words when she got drunk. "I think there are more effectual ways to spend our time and resources than fistfighting aliens."

Her eyes clouded over.

"But where are you going?"

"I don't know . . ." And then she added, almost as an afterthought, as she evaporated into nothingness, "Maybe I'll go to grad school."

Clay shook his head. "Of *course* Iris would flake out on us like that. This is bullshit. This whole goddamn thing is a high fucking tower of bullshit." He absorbed the density of the marble counter-top, punched a hole in the wall, and headed out toward the weight room.

Mutt immediately went into full damage-control mode. "Okay," he started spinning, "a press release. If Clay won't apologize, we need to distance ourselves, protect the organization. Talking points—his actions do not represent the, um, the et cetera of the Up-and-Comers, the *ideals* . . ."

I took off my necklace, the source of all my power, and placed it on the counter.

"I think I'm done," I said. "I think the Up-and-Comers are done."

Mutt shook his head. "Honey, no. You're a superhero. That's what you do."

"It's not worth it," I said.

"So what am *I* supposed to do?" Mutt pulled a contract out of his briefcase and pointed to an underlined string of legalese. "If you stop performing 'consistent acts of public heroism' we are in breach. Is that what you want? For us to get married and immediately fall into the red? You and me, without jobs, scrambling to stay out of debt, like every other fucking schmo on the planet? Is that the life you want?"

"No," I said. "It isn't."

I took off my engagement ring. I tried to crush it between my fingers, but I no longer had the strength. So instead, I just put it down on the counter next to my necklace and left.

"Wait," said Mutt. "You can't just walk away."

But as it turned out, I could do all sorts of incredible things.

Lizzy followed me out of the building.

"Hey—" she said, and I turned around.

"You were right. Is that what you want to hear? I never should have gotten engaged to Mutt. You were right. You're always right. Is that what you want me to say?"

Lizzy shook her head. "Haven't you learned by now that I never know what the fuck I'm talking about?"

I laughed. "You know, you could have told me that three years ago and saved us both a lot of time."

"Are you okay?" she asked.

"I think so," I said. "I mean, the hard part's over, right?"

And she said, "Yeah. The hard part's over."

Well, the next six months were incredibly hard, what with all the lawsuits and countersuits and breaches of contract and all that. I feel like in those six months I probably spent more time in depositions than not in depositions.

I lost my apartment in the city and moved back to my parents' house in Tulsa for a little bit—just long enough to get back on my feet. It was nice to get away from things for a second, to spend some time with my family and dry out a little. I did some temp work at my dad's office and volunteered at the Children's Theater, playing piano for their various *Guys and Dolls*es and *Damn Yankees*es.

As Lizzy would say, "Time stumbles on, in Time's dumbass way."

There were certain things I missed about the city. I missed the pancakes at Boogaloos and hikes up to Lands End. I missed propelling myself with photon blasts high up above the city to watch the sunset. Sometimes it felt like if I got myself high enough, the sun would never dip below the horizon, but of course it always did.

But mostly I missed Lizzy and all our stupid conversations about nothing in diners and how when I was around her, I didn't just like her—I liked me.

Lizzy actually came to visit me a couple weeks ago. She was driving across the country, taking her aunt's car to North Carolina, and she stopped in Tulsa and we got a coffee at Foolish Things. It was good to see Lizzy. Hanging out with her took me back in a weird sort of way, like it made me feel both young and old at the same time. It was really trippy to think there was a time not all that long ago when the most important thing in the world seemed to be stopping Doctor Tormentus from unlocking the cosmic power of the Supremacy Belt. Like, it felt like if we could just do *that,* then maybe everything would be okay. Like, man, how young were we, right?

After coffee, Lizzy had a couple hours to kill before her AA meeting, so I brought her back to my parents' house.

"Since when do you play this?" she asked, nodding at the guitar in my room.

I picked it up. "See, you think you know everything about me, but there's actually a lot you don't know."

Lizzy dropped onto my bed and smiled. "Of *course* you would keep this a secret. Has anyone ever told you you're incredible?"

I rolled my eyes. "Only everybody."

"Play me something."

I started tuning. "What do you want me to play?"

"Why don't you play me something you wrote?"

"No, I don't want to do that."

"Hey, how come you never wrote any songs for the band? Were you holding out on us?"

I concentrated on my tuning. "I didn't need to write songs; everyone else wrote songs."

"That's right," she said. "I wrote songs, Joelle wrote songs . . . How come you never brought in any songs?"

"I don't know. I just didn't."

"I'll bet you wrote some good ones; you just never brought them in."

"No . . ."

Lizzy leaned back against the headboard and closed her eyes. "Play me one of your songs, Lauren . . ."

I remember one time I asked Iris if she was afraid to die. This was when we were trapped in the Man-Pig Pit of Dimension K and it really looked like we might not make it home. Iris said, afraid or not, it didn't really matter. That the thing about death is that it's terrifying and overwhelming and it can happen at any moment. And when we're confronted with death we can either be cowardly or we can be brave, but either way we're going to die, so . . .

And I thought, Whoa, that's dark.

But here I was, sitting in my childhood bedroom with a guitar. The Up-and-Comers were over and done with and it was just Lizzy and me and it was the afternoon and it was summer in Tulsa and Lizzy was lying on my bed, looking as calm and beautiful as I had ever seen her, and she was asking me to play her something I had written.

And I thought about how, actually, if you wanted to, you could say the same thing about life. That *life* is terrifying and overwhelming and it can happen at any moment. And when you're confronted with life you can either be cowardly or you can be brave, but either way you're going to live.

So you might as well be brave.

Move across the country.

Move across the country and hope the Sadness won't find you, won't follow you like a stray dog from coast to coast. Hope the Sadness isn't just a fog on a leash, shadowing you always. Hope the Sadness can't be as fleet as you are, hope the Sadness is more rooted. Perhaps the Sadness has friends, a family, and can't just pick up and go. Look at all this stuff the Sadness has here in San Jose or Chapel Hill or wherever you're currently leaving. How's the Sadness going to survive without all this stuff? Hope this isn't one of those any-place-I-hang-my-hat-is-home-type situations where the Sadness hangs its hat on you. Hope that you are not the Sadness's home, anywhere you go, no matter how far, no matter how quickly—the Sadness lives in you. Hope to God it's not that.

Move across the country and start a new adventure. Create a brand-new life, buy a new set of furniture, a fresh autumn coat. Fill your days with distraction. Take a class, learn an instrument, visit your local library and crack open one of those Brontë sisters you always meant to get acquainted with, anything to make the days pass faster, to accumulate distance, to get you as far away as possible from the day that you left.

Move across the country and watch the short yellow lines shoot past you down the pavement. See the city recede in the distance behind the taped-up boxes obstructing your rearview. Settle somewhere fertile, plant a new you and watch you blossom. You can barely remember that old you now, the you who lived in that other place and was Sad. That old you wasn't you; *this* is you. This is the you you want to be.

You have friends now, a routine, a coffee shop where someone, as you saunter in, smiles and says, "The usual?" One night at a bar, late, you pick up a hobby of a person that somehow grows into a habit—a person whose flaws sparkle off yours in glorious coruscating patterns; a person who gets to know not just the you you sometimes show, but the you you truly are; a person who—when you weren't looking—slipped a naked, wounded heart into the pocket of your jacket with a bow and a note that said, "handle with care."

One night, you will wake with a start in this person's bed, you will discover yourself in this person's arms, and you will disentangle yourself for the hundredth time and dress yourself for the hundredth time and try to leave this person's apartment, but when you get to the door there will be a sticky note over the knob that says, "but what if this time you stayed?"

And you will turn around and get back into that person's bed, and you will get back into that person's arms, and you will stay there for a year and a half. And you will learn how to be very, very tender with that person's naked, wounded heart.

And when the Sadness catches up, tracks you down—when you return home one day, arms full of groceries, to find the Sadness sitting at the kitchen table, casually reading a paper as if it never left, eating a muffin as if this were all perfectly natural—when the Sadness looks up at you and says, "What did you think, buddy? What did you think was going to happen?"—when the Sadness smirks at you and says with a wry insistence that unravels you in an instant, "This is the real love story here, buddy, you and me"—when the Sadness reiterates that, sure, certain smaller sadnesses dull, but *this* Sadness, *the* Sadness, has seen you through it all; *this* Sadness, *the* Sadness, has never strayed from your side, not really, and why would you want it to now, this epitome of stability in an inconsistent world?—when that happens, you can put your groceries down and walk back out the door and close the door behind you.

You can get in your car and drive all night and call your person from the road and say, "I'm sorry."

You can keep driving until you hit a HELP WANTED sign dangling off the edge of the opposite coast. You can take the new job and get all your stuff shipped out to you or thrown in the garbage or thrown in the river or burned in a fire or donated to the Goodwill.

Go for a hike along the water and breathe in the fresh sea air.

Move across the country and start again someplace new.

YOU WANT TO KNOW
WHAT PLAYS ARE LIKE?

Here is my impression of a play:

Okay, so first you gotta imagine it's a hotel room, right? Just a normal, boring-looking hotel room, on the nice end of things, as far as hotel rooms go. And the audience is coming in, and they're taking their seats in this dinky little theater in lower Manhattan, barely bigger than a Winnebago, this theater, with seats that feel like someone just glued down some thin fabric over a block of hard metal. The main thing of a theater—like the whole point of it—is that there's going to be a lot of sitting in it, so you'd think they would at least consider investing in some comfortable chairs. Word to the wise: if they can't even get that part right, which absolutely most of the time they cannot, then buckle the fuck up, because I can tell you right now you are in for an ordeal of an evening.

Anyway, the people are walking down the aisle, trying to find their row, which is pretty much impossible, because even though there are only three rows in the theater, they're labeled like ROW A, ROW JJ, and ROW 2A AND A HALF, and everyone's looking at their ticket like, "I'm supposed to be in row twelve. Where the hell is twelve?" But anyway, they're walking down the aisle—and the carpet has a weird bump in it that everyone needs to be careful not to trip over—and they sit down and they look at the stage and they see a bed and a chair and a minibar, and they say, "Okay, so I guess this play takes place in a hotel room."

Half of all plays ever written take place in hotel rooms just about, so it's not a huge shock, and half of *those* are about guys on business trips spilling their guts to hookers who, it turns out, are actually really sweet. This play is not about that, but for a second it feels like it could be. Like when the audience comes in and they see the hotel room, they have to check their programs, because it's like, "Oh shit, is this going to be another one of those plays about a sad guy and a sensitive hooker, and the guy doesn't even want to have sex with her, he just wants to talk? But then later, they have sex anyway, and she doesn't even charge him, because it turns out they fell in love? And of course the hooker takes her bra off, right when she's facing the audience? God, this isn't going to be one of those plays, is it?"

So then everyone's looking at the program, right? To try to figure out whether it's one of those hooker plays. And they're reading the notes from the artistic director or whatever, and the cast bios, and it's like, "Ooh, did you see this actress played a dead body on a *Law & Order* once?" And there's a thing in the back about how we need you to donate money to the theater, like how Theater is so Vital and Important, like as if you didn't spend your money already on a ticket just to be here. Like as if they're doing you a favor to show you this play. Like as if the play-writer's parents hadn't already spent thousands of dollars to send this guy to a fancy liberal arts college so he could learn how to write plays good.

As if his big sister didn't just drive all the way down from Syracuse to be here, leaving the kids with her dirtbag ex-husband, who you just *know* is going to say some dumb shit that traumatizes them while she's gone or he's going to show them a dead cat in the alley or some old wrestling videos or something, and when she gets back she's going to get a call from the school because her kids won't stop meat-hooking and pile-driving everybody.

But anyway, the play. So the lights go down and the fancy play-bellhop comes to the front of the audience to make an announcement. And the announcement is basically: "Hey! Dummies! Turn off your cell phones! You're at a play!" But then also maybe there's a part about how this theater company has more plays coming up, and if you like plays, maybe you could buy tickets to see some more of them! And it's just like Jesus, Play, maybe for one second you could stop trying to sell me on the Concept of Plays; if I want to see more theater I know how to do it, but anyway I don't even really live here; I'm just trying to be a good older sister to my idiot play-writer brother—who, by the way, couldn't even get me into this play for free. This is another true fact about plays, which is that on top of everything else, you have to pay for your own ticket, because I guess that's what being supportive is. Because I guess if *you're* not buying a ticket, who is? Mom and Dad? Yeah, right. As the fancy play-bellhop walks back up the aisle (stumbling over the weird bump in the carpet), you look around at your fellow audience members in this half-empty theater and you wonder if the only reason any play is ever successful at all is just on account of friends and family "being supportive."

So then the play starts and the first thing that happens is two ladies burst into the hotel room, one after another. These ladies are supposed to be sisters, probably, because when plays aren't about hookers, ninety percent of the time they're about sisters. But, of course, because it's a play, these sisters look nothing alike. For starters, one of them's like fifty and the other one's like twenty, because apparently when you're hiring people for plays, it's impossible to find two women who are about the same age.

The older one goes right for the minifridge and pulls out a bottle of white wine, even though since it's a play, the white wine is actually water, if there's even something in the bottle at all, which—spoiler alert for all plays—there probably isn't. The younger lady kicks off her shoes and jumps onto the bed. And they start talking in that very fast, stutter-y I'm-a-character-in-a-play way that guys who write plays think is naturalistic, even though nobody actually talks that way except for people who just tried cocaine for the first time.

"Okay, okay, but can we— Okay, but can we talk?" says the one on the bed.

"Drink first, then talk."

"Virginia, can we *talk*, though? Can we talk, Virginia?"

People are always saying each other's names in plays. That's like the number one thing that happens in plays, is people just wedging names into sentences.

"You think I don't want to talk, Maggie? I am well aware there are things about which we need to *talk*."

"She's pretty."

"Am I drinking yet?"

"But she is pretty. You have to give her that."

"Well, of course she's pretty, Maggie. This is Dennis we're talking about. You think he's just going to date some old possum that fell off the back of a truck full of boots?"

This gets a big laugh from the audience, and it's like: Why? And I'll tell you why. It's because the standards for comedy in plays are very low. Like if you heard someone say that in a movie, you'd be like, "Where is the joke?" But I guess because this is a play and, damn it, it's out there doing the best it can, we're all just willing to meet it halfway and laugh at some of its words.

Meanwhile, it is completely unclear how old the sisters are supposed to be, but if you had to guess you'd say they're probably in their twenties, because apparently the older sister is supposed to be you, and the younger sister is supposed to be Shannon, and so it would be pretty weird if the younger character was any older than twenty-six, because that's how old Shannon was when she died.

As soon as you realize the sisters are supposed to be you and Shannon, the bottom of your heart falls out and everything inside your heart spills into the lower half of your body. At first, you think maybe the characters are just *inspired* by *certain aspects* of you and Shannon, but the more you watch, the more you realize, no, the older sister is you, cutting and callous and cruel, and the younger sister is Shannon, as Shannon as anyone has been since the real Shannon overdosed six years ago.

And the "Dennis" the sisters are talking about is your little brother, Dusty, the play-writer, and the "pretty girl" is his ex-fiancée, Tiny, and this play is from when you all went to Niagara for your parents' anniversary, which, by the way, Dusty did not tell you that's what the play was about, but to be fair, he did send you a link to a website, and you did not click on the link, so maybe this one's on you.

Anyway, "Dennis" enters soon with his girlfriend, "Tracy," and the whole rest of the play takes place in this one hotel room,

because God forbid the theater uses some of the money
it's making off its "proud sponsors" (which is just like a real
estate firm where one of the actors' dads works) to pay for a
second set.

And the character based on you is loud and cynical and the
character based on Shannon is sweet and goofy and full of energy.
And the character based on Dusty is awkward and neurotic, much
more awkward and neurotic than Dusty really is, but the character
is neurotic in a cute way, which Dusty is not. Like, for example,
it's cute for someone to be tongue-tied around his own girlfriend
because he's thinking of proposing. It's not cute for someone to
write a play about his family and then not tell his family. It's not
cute to make his sister do the five-hour drive down to New York
City and get a room at a hotel (because God knows she's not
sleeping on his filthy couch again) and buy a ticket to see his play
and then, SURPRISE—and also, BY THE WAY, the character
based on you is an alcoholic. And the character based on Shannon
is addicted to pills, which you can tell by the way she keeps taking
pills. Like as if it was obvious at the time, like as if any rational
person could've seen it, could've said something—but of course
it wasn't obvious, because if it was obvious, you would have said
something, would have done something. Of course you would
have.

And as you watch this weird mirror version of your family trip
to Niagara and you hear people around you laughing at the "jokes"
and disparagingly murmuring their judgy little murmurs, you
begin to feel very, very naked and exposed. You feel like you're a
record store full of strangers; here they go, ambling up your aisles,
riffling through your stacks. The Museum of You is now open
for business, every piece of you hung up on a wall, laid bare on a
table, harshly lit and awkwardly described. It's like one of those

dreams, is what it's like. You know the kind of dreams I'm talking about? It's like one of those.

This is a feeling that happens sometimes when you go to see plays.

So, anyway, after a full act of *that,* the lights come up and it's intermission, so you get to take a quick break before another full act of *that,* and your brother turns to you and says, "What do you think so far?"

And you say, "I'm still processing it," which is a thing you can say about plays, which means "I don't like it."

And Dusty says, "Yeah, I know it's a lot to process."

And you say, "I gotta go pee."

You go out to the lobby, and there's a line for the ladies' room about a thousand miles long, and it's like, how is this possible when there is literally almost zero people attending this play? And of course there's no line for the men's room, and you would think this is a problem that plays could have figured out by now, considering this always happens at plays. You decide to just use the men's room, and if anyone gives you a hard time about it, you can just tell them the play-writer is your brother. If anyone gives you a hard time you can say, "You know the drunk sister? In the play? That's me."

Nobody gives you a hard time.

After the bathroom, you decide you want a glass of wine and some peanut M&M's, but the line is long at the bar too, and for a moment you consider cutting to the front and making a big scene—because what are they going to do, kick you out?—but you don't want to embarrass Dusty like that (even though he clearly has no qualms about embarrassing you), so instead you go outside and call your dirtbag ex-husband.

"How are the kids?" you say.

"Kids are great—Cody, put down that blowtorch!"

You'd roll your eyes if you still had any eye rolls left for this guy—if your five years of marriage hadn't left your eyes completely depleted of rolls.

"You're hilarious, but I'd better get them back with all their fingers."

"Sure, sure. And if you're lucky, maybe I'll even throw in a couple extra fingers, just because I like you."

"You're not letting them drink soda, are you?"

Because of course your natural response to affection is criticism. Of course it is. Isn't that so like your character, after all? Isn't that what "Virginia" would do?

You can hear your ex-husband tense up over the phone. There's a pause just long enough for an implied "Not this again," and then he says, "How's the play?"

Because of course his natural response to criticism is to change the subject.

"It's about us," you say. "The whole thing's about us."

"What, us? You and me?"

"No, not you, dumbass, me and Dusty and Shannon."

"Shit, really? What *about* you and Dusty and Shannon?"

"I don't know, man. How we're all a bunch of assholes?"

"Jesus," says your dirtbag ex-husband. "Of course fucking Dusty would do this to you."

"Yeah."

"Did you know?"

"No, I didn't fucking know—are you kidding? You think I would've come down here?"

"You know, this is what he does. He pushes people away. And then he's surprised when like your parents don't wanna—"

"It's just intermission. I gotta go back in before it starts again."

"No. Dakota. Go back to the hotel, or go to a bar or something. You don't need to put yourself through that."

But of course, you do.

On the way back in, you get a glass of wine. The theater can't legally sell you the wine because it doesn't have a liquor license, but the "suggested donation" is seven dollars. You take the suggestion under consideration but ultimately decide to donate nothing, because isn't just being here donation enough?

Act two starts and the two sisters burst into the room again and the character based on Shannon kicks off her shoes again, and this time one goes flying and hits the fake wall of the hotel room and the whole set kind of wobbles a little and the audience laughs, but you are furious. You imagine your brother in rehearsal with this actress, showing her exactly how to kick off her shoes in the same way Shannon used to every time she entered a room. And it's not like that was some big family secret or something, the way she kicked off her shoes, but it feels to you that the act of re-creating it somehow degrades it. Like the next time you think about Shannon kicking off her shoes, will you be thinking of Shannon? Or will you be thinking of this actress?

The second half of the play is much weirder than the first half—part of it might be a dream, but it's kind of hard to say. At one point the lights go all red and the actors turn out to the audience and talk in unison in a weird monotone. This is a thing that happens in plays sometimes when the director is worried that the audience might be getting bored, so he makes the actors look directly at them so they get self-conscious and have to pay attention. There's a strobe light and a fog machine, and late in the show, a cup gets knocked off a table and rolls off the stage and one of the actors has to chase it into the audience, which is also a thing that happens sometimes in plays.

Then at the end there's a blackout, and your brother starts clapping immediately, like before anyone has a chance to breathe, even, like as if he's afraid that if he doesn't start clapping, nobody else would. Maybe no one would know the play's over, like. Maybe you'd all just sit there in the dark, thinking, What happened to the play? Is it going to start again? Is this part of it?

Personally, you wouldn't mind a moment—a silent moment, in the dark—to think about what you just saw, to think about what you're going to say, to decide whether you want your brother to see you crying. Most plays would probably be better if they gave you a second to collect yourself at the end, but most plays don't, and this play doesn't.

The lights come back on and the actors take their bows, and the weirdest part is that you clap for them. You find yourself applauding for this broad burlesque puppet show of your life, as if you really found the whole thing to be a marvelous endeavor. You will think about this night a lot in the months ahead, and the one thing you will ask yourself over and over is: Why did you clap?

After the play, your brother wants you to come to dinner with him and the cast and crew. Apparently, in New York, "dinner" is a meal you eat at eleven o'clock. I guess when you're an artist you can afford to take creative license with certain concepts, especially when you don't have a job to be at in the morning, or a family, or any shame about showing up at a diner at almost midnight for "dinner" and then ordering waffles.

Anyway, all the people from the play are very excited to meet Dusty's sister.

"So you're the real Virginia," says the actress who played Virginia.

"Actually, I'm Dakota," you say. "I'm pretty sure Virginia's based on our other sister Massachusetts."

"Oh, is that the one who passed away?" says the actress.

And Dusty says, "She's joking. We don't have a sister named Massachusetts."

Then everyone ignores you for a little bit, because they're show folk, and show folk think that what makes a good conversation is each of them taking turns just saying their funny stories at the room for a half hour. This is the most brutal part, honestly—that after you just spent two and a half hours watching their show, they took you to a second location where there's more show.

Eventually, after they get tired of talking about themselves, the theater people are ready to hear *you* talk about themselves, and one turns to you and says, "Dakota, what did you think of the play?"

You finish your beer and say, "I thought it was unrealistic that at the end, they all confront the sister about the pills. Didn't feel real to me."

Everyone gets all awkward. The actress who played Tracy laughs because she thinks you're joking, but then when she sees that no one else is laughing she says, "Excuse me," and she gets up from the table and you never see her again for the rest of your life.

Your brother shakes his head. "Jesus Christ, Dakota, it's a play."

"I'm just saying it didn't feel real."

Then the director says something like, "I understand what's happening here. You see, Dakota, in fiction, sometimes things can play out counterfactually—or differently to the way they did in real life, and the difference between the two is what gives the fiction its vibrancy."

And you say, "Oh, wow, really? Is that how fiction works?

I didn't fucking know that, about fiction being counterfactual and all. Thank you for elucidating to me what fiction is."

And your brother says, "Dakota, calm down."

"Why? Am I embarrassing you?"

"Yeah, actually."

"So, just to be clear, this is embarrassing? Everything in that play—all the dirty laundry—that's, what, fiction? But *this* is embarrassing."

And all the theater people avert their eyes because they're real uncomfortable that they're for a moment not the center of attention, and Dusty says, "Can I talk to you outside?"

So you go outside and you light a cigarette, and a man with the restaurant says, "Excuse me, ma'am, you can't smoke within fifteen feet of the outdoor seating area," and if that isn't the most bullshit part of all of this, then I don't know what.

"What's going on?" says Dusty.

You shake your head, because if he doesn't know by now, what the fuck?

"Look," he says, "I know that was rough to sit through, but how do you think I feel? I've been working on this play for the last year and a half."

You snort. Boy, isn't that something?

A bus goes by with an ad on the side for a play—a real play, on Broadway—and you wonder if every play—every piece of narrative "fiction"—is just some excuse for the guy who wrote it to talk some shit.

"Who said that's okay?" you ask. "The stuff you put in that show, who gave you permission?"

Dusty looks at his feet. "Look, when you're an artist, it's all grist for the mill."

"No. I'm not your 'grist.' Shannon is not 'grist.' You need to deal with your shit."

"I am trying to deal with it. This is how I'm dealing with it."

You can't look at him now, because if you do you'll start crying. You should probably just drop it there, but instead you say, "Yeah? And are you also dealing with how I'm a bad mother? And an alcoholic? Is that all stuff you need to deal with in your play?"

"When did I say you're a bad mother?"

"You think I'm a bad mother because I dropped Taylor on the head once." And now you are crying, which is—forget what I said earlier—the actual most bullshit part of all of this.

"What are you talking about?"

"You put it in your play that I dropped Taylor on the head, and it's a big joke, and everyone's laughing, and I'm sitting there thinking, All these people think I'm a bad mother."

"Did you drop Taylor on the head? I just made that up, it wasn't about you."

"But the whole thing was about me. And Shannon. And you, and Mom and Dad. And how we're all bad people because we didn't save her."

And then you can tell Dusty wants to say something, but then he thinks better of it, but then after a moment of silence, he can't help himself and says it anyway: "Well, we didn't save her, did we?"

Oh, I forgot to mention earlier—another stupid thing about plays is that sometimes there's a sound effect of a phone ringing, and it keeps going for a beat even after the actor answers the phone. It's pretty funny when that happens.

Okay, what was I talking about?

Right, outside the restaurant. Okay.

Okay.

"Dusty," you say, "we didn't know. There was nothing we could do."

And now he's getting angry: "Really? You didn't know? When we went to Niagara and she kept slipping off to the bathroom all weekend? When she kept falling asleep at the dinner table—when she would giggle for a half hour and touch everyone's face—none of that was suspicious to you?"

"I just thought she was being goofy—she was being Shannon."

"Yeah, she was being Shannon, because Shannon was an addict."

"And you're saying if I wasn't such a drunk I would have noticed. You think Shannon overdosed because I—"

"I'm just saying it was obvious. All weekend Tiny kept saying, 'What's going on with your sister?'"

"Well, I'm sorry I'm not as astute an observer of human behavior as Tiny is. If it was so obvious to you, why didn't you say something?"

"I don't know," he says, and he chokes out the next line like it's snagged on a hook in his throat: "I will never know."

You feel bad, but then you feel angry at him for making you feel like that, when he's the one who should feel bad after the stunt he pulled, so you say, "Shannon is not your story to tell. I am not your story to tell."

And he says, "I'm sorry you feel that way."

You nod. That's basically what you're going to get from Dusty; I don't know why you thought you'd get anything different.

"I'm going back to the hotel," you say. "How much do I owe you for dinner?"

And he says, "Don't worry about it."

And you say, "No, come on, let me pay."

And he says, "No. Don't worry about it."

So, good, I guess. One less thing to worry about.

You start to walk away, and Dusty calls out, "I guess it's a good thing Mom and Dad didn't come, right? They would have hated it."

You turn back. "I don't know, man. I don't even know what they're about anymore."

If there's one silver lining to the cloud of shit that was tonight, it's that at least the play wasn't about what happened *after* Shannon died, about how your parents retreated into themselves, cut their losses—how when you tried to call them, your mother said, "I'm sorry, Dakota, talking to you . . . it's just too much for us right now"—how when she said that, your own grief tripled. You don't think you could stand to see a play about that.

"I sent them an email, but . . . I don't know why I thought they would come."

You look at him. And the play version of you would hug him. The play version of you would say, "Dusty. Whatever is going on with those two, I promise you it is not your fault."

But the real version of you just looks at him and offers a sympathetic little nothing of shrug, which somehow is supposed to communicate all the things that need to be communicated.

And he says, "Well. Thanks for coming."

You go back to your hotel room, by yourself, and head straight for the minifridge and pull out the bottle of wine you bought earlier.

The room has two beds, because you couldn't get one with just one bed, and you wish Shannon could be there. For all of it, actually, you wish Shannon could've been there. You would have liked to hear what she had to say about the play, so even just for that.

You know it wouldn't have bothered her the way it bothered you, which is also pretty annoying, because why do you always have to be the one who gets bothered by things? After dinner with Dusty, you'd go out for drinks, just you two, and after drinks you'd head back to the hotel room that you were sharing and Shannon would kick off her shoes.

"I liked it," she'd say, which of course would drive you crazy.

At the very least, Shannon would've gotten a kick out of the fact that the actress who played her was on a *Law & Order* once. "Fancy," she would say. And she'd look at you all smug, like this was some great achievement on her part. This would bug you at the time, but looking back at it, you'd think it was hilarious. For months afterward, you'd think back on this moment—Shannon saying, "Fancy," and sitting up straight in her seat like the goddamn Duchess of Wales—and it would make you smile every time.

So even just for that.

the poem

"I'm more than a little ambivalent over expressions
    of tender devotion
This one day a year because greeting card companies
    profit off store-bought emotion.
A romance-industrial complex so fueled by commodification
    of feeling
Serves only to further homogenize all and promote what's,
    at best, unrevealing.

It's not just a lack of precision—this one-size-fits-allness—
    that leads me to mope.
I think you and I share the same disillusionment,
    sprouted from long-buried hope.
I worry, as you do, love dulls us to cold hollow sockets
    that ache for a joint.
If ends are encoded in every beginning, we wonder,
    then what is the point?

You're right to be highly suspicious of seemingly mandated
  acts of affection,
When all pretty words are a means to an ultimate heartbreak,
  a grand misdirection.
I can't guarantee that this letter won't lead to us both
  one day broken and blue.
All that being said, though? You turn me to mush.
  Happy Valentine's, Wendy, to you."

As Wendy regarded the card she received with a coolness that
  trended toward frozen,
Fernando now briefly considered he'd gone a bit wrong with
  the words he had chosen.
He'd wanted to offer assurance to Wendy that all her
  concerns were well founded,
While also affirming he wasn't afraid of the many alarm bells
  she'd sounded.

"Hey, don't fall in love with me," Wendy had said,
  and Fernando insisted, "I'm not!"
He thought he had threaded the needle quite well,
  but it seemed not as well as he'd thought.
"You turn me to mush" was perhaps a bit much—
  yes, in hindsight his error was here;
The poem's detachment undone in an instant by something
  so baldly sincere.

For years, he'd been grasping at chances for subtle advances,
    and now he was handing
His heart in a card to this woman, her glances askance
    at romance notwithstanding.
"It's clever," she said, as she folded the note. "If there's one thing
    I've noticed, you're clever."
He smiled, forgetting again his endeavor to be more blasé
    and whatever.

When Wendy had called him to give him the word her
    engagement with Warren was broken,
Implied in that word—or at least what he'd heard—
    was an offer, inferred but not spoken.
And when Wendy wandered from Williamsburg just to wind up
    at Fernando's in Queens?
And crawled into bed with him? Turned off her phone?
    Well, I think we all know what *that* means.

The fact that she'd stayed for two weeks with no mention
    of how long she planned to be crashing
Was fine with her host, who supplied her with hugs and two mugs:
    one for wine, one for ashing.
He grew quite accustomed to making her breakfast,
    to being her number one man,
To squeezing her hand as she cried on the phone to her mom,
    "No, I don't think I can!"

The present was messy; the past a disaster; the future,
    however, was clear—
Except for the future of two days away, because Valentine's Day
    was now near.
He knew that he had to be gentle, not too sentimental,
    romantic, or rote,
But somehow he felt like he had to do *something,*
    and something was writing this note.

He tried to be slightly sardonic—just slightly—without coming
    off as sarcastic.
He mainly just wanted his still fragile houseguest to know
    she was frankly fantastic.
Though Wendy's heart would not unshatter, Fernando could help
    piece together the shards.
"But I thought we had an agreement," said Wendy. "Like didn't
    I tell you no cards?"

Fernando debated explaining that this was an *anti*-card,
    that was the joke.
Like what do you get for the girl who wants nothing
    but fucking and more Diet Coke?
A cynical love poem slathered in brine with the tiniest dollop
    of honey—
But then he thought maybe it's one of those things—
    if you have to explain, it's not funny.

Instead he said, "Sorry, I guess it was stupid, I just got
    a little excited."
And Wendy felt bad that she made him feel sad and decided
    this wrong would be righted.
"I love it," she lied, and she tried to look happy, though truly
    the whole thing was frightening.
Engaged in escaping the knots of her past, she'd been blind
    to the new noose now tightening.

Fernando was kind, he was handsome and witty,
    and there when she'd needed him most,
But Wendy now worried she'd quite inadvertently smitten
    her love-bitten host.
And yes, Wendy liked him, and true, she had privately
    pictured the boyfriend he'd make,
But still she knew letting this fling now spin into a *thing* was
    a deadly mistake.

For starters, she'd just left a man at the altar; if anything,
    she needed space.
But how do you keep a straight face when you say, "I need space,"
    while you crash at his place?
You put on his sweater, you sleep in his arms—well, that carries,
    perhaps, implication,
Abetted by joint expectation, the anticipation from years
    of flirtation.

And then add two weeks' worth of kissing, and drinking,
    and sharing the scars of their youth—
She'd climbed in his heart without thinking, the way that a kid idly
    tongues a loose tooth.
The truth was that even though she and Fernando could be
    a good thing for a minute,
The month she had planned to get married was maybe not
    quite the right month to begin it.

On top of all that, though, assuming the two could have worked
    through the terrible timing,
It still felt presumptuous to write her a poem. Like, why did he
    think she liked rhyming?
If truly Fernando had felt a connection, then couldn't
    Fernando intuit
That if his intention was wooing this woman, this wasn't
    a good way to do it?

The poem was clever, but cloyingly so, overflowing with
    whimsy and vim.
So, was it for her, as the verses asserted, or was it, in fact,
    more for him?
Fernando's affection felt clingy but distant—familiar,
    yet still somehow foreign.
(Besides, if she'd wanted unyielding devotion, she could have
    just never left Warren.)

"I'm sorry," Fernando suggested but didn't quite say, in regards
    to the letter.
And even though Wendy insisted he shouldn't feel bad,
    he felt worse—he knew better.
The poem was maybe a little indulgent, a maudlin emotional
    jack-off.
He'd meant to be playful and fun—Dr. Seuss!—only now
    things felt more David Rakoff.

And so they both sat for a moment in stillness, the silence
    beginning to pool;
Each one of them struck by the notion their actions had not
    just been selfish, but cruel.
Fernando thought maybe he still had a chance to say something
    profound and specific.
Instead he said, "Hey, so, the thing of it all is, you know,
    I just think you're terrific?"

"This isn't . . ." said Wendy, and then she trailed off,
    and Fernando said, "Yeah, no, I get it.
I guess I just thought it was better to say than to not
    and then later regret it."
And Wendy said, "Yeah . . ." and Fernando remembered
    the first time he'd mentioned to friends
The current arrangement and one of them said,
    "Well, I can't wait to see how *this* ends!"

His sister had told him, "Be careful, you know what they say:
    Roaming hearts gonna roam."
So now he was less than astonished when Wendy said, "Honestly?
    I should go home."
Fernando said nothing, for what could be said? It was over
    and done with, and soon
His half-a-month lover would just disappear in the folds
    of the cold afternoon.

He threw all his sheets in the laundry and stared straight ahead,
    less perturbed than perplexed.
As Wendy awaited her subway, she found Warren's number
    and crafted a text.
A poem's a thing that is hard to pin down, though the words
    pile up in your head.
A person's a thing that is tricky to read, but it's trickier
    yet to feel read.

THE AVERAGE
of All Possible
Things

Lucinda, the average of all possible things, woke up very averagely in her extremely unexceptional apartment. She put on some very normal clothes, glanced at her mirror, which was just the regular amount of reflective, as far as mirrors go, and as she looked at her quite average self, she thought: Yeah, okay.

She got in her car (which was fine) and drove to her job (which was fine). Everything was beige, and stucco, and fine. It was a very normal day, like pretty much any other, the only notable thing at all about it being that at one point she didn't look at her phone for a whole eight minutes.

She ate lunch by herself at her desk. Kale Caesar salad and a club soda.

The thermostat was set to seventy-one degrees.

That night, she returned to her extremely unexceptional apartment. For dinner, she reheated some pasta she'd made for herself the night before—it wasn't great, but it wasn't bad either. She ate a normal-sized serving, then watched two and a half hours of home renovation shows while replying to work emails, then went to bed.

She had trouble falling asleep at first, so she counted down from three hundred by sevens, then eights, then nines. At 3:32 a.m., she checked to see if she'd gotten any text messages—but of course she had not because it was 3:32 a.m. It was very normal to not receive text messages at 3:32 a.m. It was normal, and fine, and what Lucinda deserved.

Lucinda woke up in the morning with a crick in her neck, which was what Lucinda deserved.

Traffic to work was normal. There was a gruesome accident on the freeway, which was statistically appropriate. The radio played eight songs that were very popular and Lucinda liked all of them but didn't love any of them, and she briefly wondered if she was incapable of loving anything ever again, which is a very normal thing for a person to briefly wonder.

When she got to work, she did not have any new text messages.

She had thirty-one new emails, but they were all either work-related or junk offers from mailing lists she had been too lazy to unsubscribe from. She briefly wondered if hundreds of years after she was gone and forgotten, her last remaining legacy would be a never-checked email account that still received dozens of messages a day from automatic email bots who had no idea she was long dead and therefore not interested in an exciting buy-one-get-one-twenty-percent-off offer from Sephora.

She ate lunch by herself. Kale Caesar salad and a club soda.

"You really love these kale Caesars," said Debbie, the receptionist, dropping off Lucinda's kale Caesar.

"Yeah, well, I like to be reminded that if you get stabbed in the heart enough times, eventually they'll name a salad after you."

This was an average joke, but Debbie laughed at it like it was above average, which was a very nice thing for her to do. Everyone was Very Nice to Lucinda these days, which only made things worse, honestly, because it meant that they *knew*. Of course they couldn't *know* know, because nobody *knew*, not really. That was part of it, both part of the good and part of the bad—the fact that nobody knew. But still, somehow people knew *something*, and that's why they were being Very Nice. Somehow there had been Conversations in the kitchen about How We Should All Be Nice to Lucinda because she's Going Through a Lot, even though Lucinda wasn't even going through all that much really, she was just going through the normal amount of stuff that everyone goes through. It was normal and boring and fine, and it sucked, but it was fine.

At 2:18 exactly, Gavin swung by her office to ask if she'd finished putting together that memo compiling all the occurrences of tech support calls during the forty-five days outlined in the class-action suit as the "Period of the Exploding Bluetooth Headphones." Lucinda said not yet but she could get it to him by the end of the hour, and she *didn't* say it was taking her longer because the new large-breasted legal assistant Gavin hired had a charming predilection for confusing area codes with zip codes—which, all things considered, was very decent of Lucinda not to say.

Gavin smiled at her, which was Very Nice, and Lucinda thought it was awfully cruel of Gavin to be so Very Nice, and Gavin said, "Thanks a lot, Lucinda."

"Of course," said Lucinda, and Gavin smiled again and walked away.

Lucinda opened up the document she'd been working on and

thought about how when Gavin said "Thanks a lot," he didn't say "Thanks a lot, Luce." He said "Lucinda," which was her name, and it sounded weird when he said it, but it shouldn't have sounded weird, because Lucinda was her name after all, and it would have been much weirder if he had said "Luce," because Luce was a name for boyfriends to call her, and Gavin was not, at that moment, her boyfriend.

Lucinda pulled out her phone and drafted a text message to Gavin: "Working on that memo now. Sorry it's taking so long, but you know koalas sleep for twenty hours a day."

She looked at the message and decided not to send it, thank God, and instead she sent a text message that said, "Sorry if that was weird."

After she sent it, she saw the three dots indicating Gavin was drafting a response, but whatever he was drafting he didn't send, and the three dots went away. Lucinda put her phone in her desk drawer and worked on the memo. At 2:42, she finished the memo but didn't want to send it without first checking to see if Gavin had responded to her text message. He hadn't. She waited until three o'clock exactly, then sent him the memo attached to an email that just said, "here you go."

Eighteen minutes later he responded with an email that said, "thanks."

She didn't look at her phone the whole time she was driving home, but when she got home Gavin still had not responded to her text message that said, "Sorry if that was weird." She thought about texting him again, "Sorry if that text message about things being weird was weird," but she didn't, thank God.

Instead she went to see a movie by herself, which is a normal thing for a single woman to do. She had trouble focusing on the movie, though, because she kept thinking about how good it was that she couldn't look at her phone during the movie, and how by the time the movie was over she would probably have a few new text messages to look at, from Gavin or anybody else who wanted to text her, but then when she turned her phone back on after the movie, she had gotten no new text messages.

That night she left her phone near her bed, but she put it on Do Not Disturb mode, so that she wouldn't get woken up if she got any new text messages, but then at midnight, she thought, This is stupid, so she turned her phone off, but then at 2:14 a.m., she thought, This is stupid, so she turned her phone back on, and sure enough she had gotten a text message from Gavin at 12:41 that said, "It wasn't weird."

And Lucinda thought: Okay. So it wasn't weird.

The next day, Lucinda was in her office, performing her job adequately, when she got a text message from a number she didn't recognize that said, "i have something for you."

When Lucinda got text messages from numbers she didn't recognize, she liked to prolong the conversation for as long as possible without asking who it was, to see if she could figure it out. This is a very normal thing unexceptional people do, because their lives aren't exciting enough in other ways so they have to create little mysteries for themselves, and since Lucinda was so unexceptional, it was quite appropriate that she did this.

"What do you have for me?" Lucinda texted back.

"it is a surprise," said the number she didn't recognize.

"Can I have a hint?"

Then Lucinda saw the three dots that meant the person was drafting a response. The three dots stayed there for exactly one minute and thirty-four seconds, and then came the response: "no."

Lucinda put her phone in the top drawer of her desk and got to work.

At twelve past eleven, Gavin swung by Lucinda's office on his way to Conference Room H. He nodded as he passed the doorway and said, "Lucinda."

Lucinda nodded back, then went to the bathroom and cried for eighteen minutes.

At lunch, Debbie dropped off a kale Caesar salad and a club soda, and then lingered for a moment.

"Thanks, Debbie," said Lucinda.

"Sure thing," said Debbie.

She continued to linger.

"Can I help you with anything else?" asked Lucinda.

"Don't you want to know what your surprise is?"

Lucinda tried to hide her disappointment in learning that the mysterious stranger she had been texting was just Debbie, the receptionist.

"Yeah," she said. "What's my surprise?"

Debbie pulled a cereal box out of her messenger bag. "I thought you might like this box of Cinnamon Sugar Blast Oat Cubes."

Lucinda looked at the box of Cinnamon Sugar Blast Oat Cubes. "Why?"

"It comes with a free Minions wristwatch."

"Oh," said Lucinda. "Cute."

Lucinda briefly wondered how old Debbie was. If she had to guess, Lucinda would say twenty-two, but she would also believe it if someone told her Debbie was a precocious fourteen or a smooth-skinned fifty-eight.

"The Minions are hilarious," said Debbie.

And Lucinda said, "I should get back to work."

"Okay," said Debbie.

Debbie left the room, leaving the box of Cinnamon Sugar Blast Oat Cubes with the free Minions wristwatch on Lucinda's desk. Lucinda nudged the box to the side with a pencil and opened Facebook on her phone. Before it could even load, she closed it again, then deleted the app. Then she opened Facebook on her computer and looked at her own profile. She still hadn't changed her profile picture, which was dumb, but she felt that changing it would be Admitting Something—not that the relationship was over (because of course it was, whether Lucinda wanted to admit it or not) but that she Cared.

The picture was of her in Hawaii, smiling wide, an arm around her waist. Whose arm was it? There was no way to tell from the picture. There was no way to tell that Lucinda had gone to Hawaii with a boyfriend over Christmas. There was no way to tell that Lucinda had a boyfriend. There was no way to tell that Gavin hadn't in fact gone back east to see his family over Christmas. There was no way to tell that for five months and eight days, two people shared something marvelous and intimate and true. There was no evidence of this ever occurring. Nobody knew. But still, in the picture, there was an arm around her waist—the arm of a man who would now never again love Lucinda and wake her up with sweet kisses and lie about going back east to see his family while spending a week with an arm around Lucinda's waist in Hawaii. Not that Lucinda Cared.

It was very important to Lucinda that everyone on Facebook understood that she hadn't bothered to change the picture yet because that's how Little she Cared, and not because she was like obsessed or something. After all, this was no tragic love story, her and Gavin, hardly the kind of thing they write great operas about. It was the kind of thing they write just okay operas about, where the audience is mostly just the friends of the guy who wrote the opera, and afterward, they're all just hanging out in the lobby trying to think of nice things to say, and then their friend comes out and they all go, "Hey! Look at you! You wrote an opera! Wow!"

What annoyed Lucinda most of all was that they still had to work together. Gavin still continued to exist in the world, which Lucinda thought was very rude.

If you were an undercover detective observing the comings and goings of Weissman, Zeitzman & Kinsey, you might suspect that Lucinda had once been in love with Gavin, but you'd never guess it was for the way that he talked to her, and how she felt when she talked to him, because now they could barely talk to each other at all. Every conversation was punctuated by long awkward silences— but punctuated the Spanish way, so every sentence was followed by a long awkward silence and preceded by the same awkward silence upside down.

And when he spoke to her, he called her "Lucinda," which sliced and gutted her every time, even though she knew that was stupid, because what else would he call her? "Luce"? No way. "Koala"? No. He used to call her a koala because of the way she wrapped herself around him in bed, like a koala on a branch. She had wrapped her whole life around him, like a koala on a branch. And now the branch was gone and Lucinda had to deal with the fact that her life was now wrapped around nothing—which of course was all perfectly normal. All the pain Lucinda now felt was normal. The emptiness was normal. The harsh incinerating boring awful raw barren obsessive numb five-hundred-volt nothingness now completely consuming her was so totally average.

Lucinda looked at her phone, just to check the time. She noticed she did not have any new text messages and put her phone in her desk drawer. She then realized she had not actually noticed the time, so she took her phone out again. She noticed that since she'd put the phone in her desk drawer a moment ago, she had not received any new text messages. She put her phone in her desk drawer again. Then she remembered that there was a clock on her computer. It was seven minutes after one. She noticed her Facebook profile was still open on her computer and she wondered how many people had just walked by her office on their way to Conference Room H and seen the picture of her in Hawaii with a mysterious man's arm around her waist.

The problem with Lucinda's office was that the walls were made of glass, and its central location meant you couldn't not look directly into it on your way to the kitchen or the bathrooms or Conference Room H. She used to like being in the center of things like this—it made her feel important. But now it just made her feel like a fish in a bowl, constantly on display. Pretty colors for the people to look at.

She deleted her Facebook account.

She decided she would not look at her phone again for another hour.

She got a lot of work done in that hour, and also got a lot of think-ing done about how much work she was doing and how good it was that she wasn't dating Gavin anymore so she could focus on her work. Before she was dating Gavin, she used to spend a good por-tion of her day thinking about excuses to go visit Gavin in his office, but now she was not thinking that, so she could really be productive.

Before she was dating Gavin, she would idle in the doorway to Gavin's office after hand-delivering him some research memo, and transform somehow from the boring Lucinda she had always been into some other Lucinda who was deliciously witty and charming, making all sorts of conversation around such scintillating topics as: *That research memo was really fun to put together,* and: *How was Gavin enjoying Colorado Springs?* and: *Since she grew up there, did he need any advice about fun things to do in the Springs?* and (when he called her bluff and said, "Yeah, what's the best thing to do in the Springs?"): *Oh, shit, uhhhh, drive somewhere else?*

And when she kissed Gavin late one night in the copy room, while the whole team was line editing some bullshit after hours so they could get it filed by midnight, and when he kissed her back, with everybody in the whole world just on the other side of a paper-thin door eating paper-thin pizza over brick-thick documents, Lucinda had felt sexy and bold and beautiful and endlessly fascinating.

And when she went home with him and then showed up to the office the next day wearing the same clothes and everybody who walked by her fishbowl office on the way to Conference Room H could see it, she had felt sexy and bold and beautiful and endlessly fascinating.

And over the next five months and eight days, when she and Gavin would drown each other in tsunamis of text messages—inside jokes and tiny observations, but also occasional admissions of "God, I couldn't pay attention during Andrea's sexual harassment presentation because the whole time I was thinking about how badly I want you to rip my clothes off and fuck me in your office"—just knowing that these messages were being transmitted in the middle of Important Meetings, whizzing past the heads of their unwitting coworkers, all of these coworkers just living their boring, average coworker lives—it all made her feel sexy and bold and beautiful and endlessly fascinating.

But now she understood that she was wrong to have felt that way, because Lucinda was not sexy and bold and beautiful and endlessly fascinating. She was regular, and average, and boring, and fine.

And she knew that now, although to be honest, secretly part of her kind of thought it all along.

Everywhere she went there were little reminders of how completely *Lucinda* she was, how unworthy of any experience approaching extraordinary. She tried to open a small carton of orange juice and she couldn't get the stupid *thing* of it to rip in the right direction and honestly why do they even still have these dumb little orange juice cartons here, like hasn't this firm ever heard of bottles? And then she ended up spilling orange juice all over her shirt and she thought: I deserve this.

At the end of the day, Debbie asked if she was staying late and needed dinner, and Lucinda said, "No."

She walked past Gavin's office, which reminded her of Gavin.

She got in the elevator, in which she had kissed Gavin at least a hundred times, and she thought about how cruel the elevator was for reminding her of that. Fucking elevator, *how dare it?*

In the garage, she passed Gavin's BMW, parked in Gavin's parking spot.

On the drive home, she passed a store with a display in front that said WE SELL BOXES, which reminded her of the time she got mad at Gavin because he was always sucking up to Harold Weissman, laughing at all his jokes.

"And by the way," Lucinda had said, "you *never* laugh at my jokes."

And Gavin had said, "That's because your idea of a joke is going into a store with a big sign out front that says WE SELL BOXES and asking the guy behind the counter, 'Excuse me, do you sell boxes?' "

"Yeah. It's hilarious when I do that."

"It was *kind of* funny the *first time* you did that."

"No. It gets funnier every time, and it's bizarre to me that you don't understand that."

Lucinda made herself a chickpea polenta for dinner and forced herself to picture Gavin at his dumbest and unsexiest, like the time they were walking to Gavin's car after lunch one day and he said, "Hey, look at this cute plant store," and Lucinda thought: Did he just call this flower shop a "plant store"?

Lucinda imagined telling that story in a speech one day, and everybody laughing. Why was she giving a speech? Where was she? It didn't matter.

"You know," Lucinda continued in her imaginary speech, "Gavin's the kind of guy who thinks hating brunch is a personality."

More laughter from the crowd. It was everyone from the office, along with all of Gavin's friends and Lucinda's friends.

"Gavin's the kind of guy who would love to go camping—he'd *looooove* to go camping, just not on any of the weekends you invite him to go camping with you, but seriously, he loves the *idea* of camping, he is definitely down to go camping with you, any day now, as long as he can bring his Tempur-Pedic mattress and white-noise machine."

The imaginary crowd erupted with laughter as Gavin forced a grin and a nod to show that he was in on the joke, but Lucinda knew that behind the smile he was steaming, the way he always silently stewed when she teased him in front of his friends.

Lucinda relished his pain, but before she could turn the screw even more, he raised his eyebrows and offered a little smirk, like, *What can I say? You got me, Luce,* and in an instant Lucinda forgave him for everything. She realizes she was wearing a wedding dress. Why? Oh no! She was giving this speech at her wedding, to Gavin! What a terrible thing to be happening! Why would her imagination do this to her?! She immediately stopped imagining.

Lucinda crawled into bed and thought about when would be a good time to quit her job. She knew she couldn't quit now because then Gavin would assume she was quitting because of the breakup, and she didn't want to give him that power.

She thought about humiliating Gavin on her way out the door, printing out all the dirty emails they'd exchanged from their work accounts and plastering the glass walls of her fishbowl office with them for everyone to see.

"What the hell is this?" Gavin would say, as his peers and mentors congregated around Lucinda's office and immersed themselves in their entire epistolary romance.

Lucinda would look at the pages on the wall and pretend to be confused. "Oh, I just wanted some privacy in my office so I covered the windows; I wasn't even paying attention to what I was printing out. Well, anyway, I quit."

"This isn't funny, Lucinda," Gavin would shout, and Lucinda would have to agree that it wasn't funny, not really. But maybe Lucinda wasn't capable of being funny anymore. Maybe Gavin was right—she was never really funny to begin with.

Lucinda imagined Gavin storming into her office to tear down the emails, and it struck her that this would be the most time Gavin had ever spent in her office. It occurred to Lucinda that throughout their affair, but also just throughout them working together, all of their major conversations had taken place in *his* office. Gavin was fond of poking his head through Lucinda's doorway to ask for a memo, or nodding at her through the glass wall on the way to Conference Room H, but all the important milestones in their sexual and/or professional relationship had taken place on his turf.

But again, her breakup with Gavin was not the *reason* she wanted to quit, which is why she couldn't quit right now, and she couldn't quit in any way that seemed to imply that the decision was even slightly inspired by Gavin.

The truth was she'd been thinking about leaving Weissman, Zeitzman & Kinsey ever since the firm made Karen Glassman a junior partner. The truth was Lucinda never even wanted to work there in the first place; she just kind of fell into the position, the same way she seemed to always just kind of fall into everything. A person as unexceptional as Lucinda doesn't live a life as much as a life just floods in around her, filling up whatever empty space a life should be occupying. She wasn't even sure she wanted to be a lawyer really—she'd just gone to Boalt because nothing else was happening for her, and she figured if she went back to school she could put off making any more decisions for at least another couple years.

Gavin always thought this was hilarious—that someone would

go to law school and take the bar just for the hell of it—and when Lucinda tried to clarify, "I didn't say it was *just for the hell of it*," Gavin said, "No, no, I get it."

And then they made Karen Glassman a junior partner.

Lucinda thought about Karen Glassman's promotion on her drive to work. She thought about Karen Glassman's promotion a lot. She actually liked Karen Glassman, personally, and she was happy for her success. There was no real reason to think about her promotion so much, other than it was easier for Lucinda to think about that than to think about the end result of Karen's promotion: Gavin and Lucinda getting in a big fight about it.

She'd asked Gavin if the partners had ever considered making *her* a junior partner, and Gavin said, "You know I can't answer that."

"Boo," Lucinda said. "What's even the point of having a secret relationship if we're not going to be spies for each other?"

Gavin bristled at the accusation, even though technically there had been no accusation—Gavin just always heard accusations in everything, which would've been a good thing for him to discuss with his therapist, if he didn't also consider it an accusation of some sort every time Lucinda suggested he see a therapist.

"The only reason we're in a secret relationship," he muttered, "is because *you* didn't want to go to HR."

"Yeah, but that's just because I wanted to work on your cases still. If we went to HR, I'd have to work for Harold or Joel, and then I'd probably kill myself, and that would be a whole other legal headache."

———

Lucinda now spent the morning trying not to think about that conversation. It was a very productive morning—she got a lot of not thinking done.

For lunch she had a kale Caesar salad.

After lunch, she shifted to not thinking about the next Karen Glassman conversation, the one that oozed out three days later because she couldn't leave well enough alone. She kept scratching at the Karen Glassman itch, sniffing around the periphery of the Karen Glassman situation, edging right up to the woods of Karen Glassman and making a camp at the entrance to those woods, and starting a fire at the camp, and baking some beans, until finally Gavin (who would *love* to go camping sometime) exploded, "Luce, drop it, you were never going to get Karen's promotion."

"Why not?"

"Come on, you can't compare yourself to Karen. She's actually looking at this as a career—she believes in the work we're doing."

"I believe in the work!"

"Luce, you know what I mean. Karen gets dinner at the office and works late every night."

"I sometimes work late!"

"No, you don't! You *used* to work late, but that was just so you could flirt with me."

"You never told me I was supposed to!"

"I'm not going to tell my *girlfriend* she has to work late. Besides, you don't even really want to be a lawyer."

"I totally do, kind of!"

"Come on. This place is a joke to you. You're always writing up jokey research memos, about like the Barenaked Ladies or whatever."

"Okay, first of all, the band is just called Barenaked Ladies, there's no 'the.'"

It's true that Lucinda had once spent hours of her own time putting together a research memo on the Canadian rock band Barenaked Ladies, specifically investigating whether then lead singer Steven Page was purposefully singing in a fake American accent for their 1998 hit single "One Week."

She'd noticed that the song loudly announces itself with the lyric "IT'S BEEN," but the word "been" is pronounced *bin,* which is the American pronunciation, as opposed to the more Canadian way of saying it, *bean.* Even more notably, the oft-repeated lyric "sorry" is also pronounced the American way, *sawry,* instead of a round Canadian *soary.*

After scouring the internet for video and audio interviews with Steven Page, she discovered that he did in fact pronounce "been" the Canadian way in casual conversation, which meant he (intentionally or not) was putting on a fake American accent when he recorded the song.

Lucinda couldn't find any literature or analysis on this subject, so she was forced to conjure her own theories, which included:

a. Steven Page was actively suppressing his Canadian accent because someone told him his music would be more successful worldwide if he sounded more American,

b. he was subconsciously suppressing his accent because he'd already internalized this idea, or

c. the song itself is sung from the point of view of a character who lives in the United States and is in fact a subtle satire of American culture.

So, yes, Lucinda had written a memo about Barenaked Ladies and distributed it to several other lawyers in the office, but that didn't mean she didn't also, when she wasn't doing that, take the job seriously.

"Plus," Gavin continued, "you're always talking shit about Joel and how handsy he is."

"That's not 'talking shit'—"

"You know what I mean."

"You think Karen Glassman never complains about Joel?"

"I'm just saying you and Karen want different things."

"You don't know that."

"Luce, be honest. If we got married tomorrow and I said you never had to work again, would you still want to be writing research memos for Weissman, Zeitzman & Kinsey?"

All the air must have gotten tremendously embarrassed and left the room, because Lucinda suddenly couldn't find any.

"What the fuck is that? A proposal?"

"No, I'm just saying."

"Saying what, that I'm not partner material because I'm wife material?"

"You know that's not what I meant."

"*Do* I know that?"

"Come on. You're tired. Let's go to bed."

Two days, eleven hours, and four minutes after that conversation, Lucinda was working on a memo on the legality of secretly serving soup with chicken stock to vegetarian homeless people, when Gavin texted her, asking if she would swing by his office.

"Could you close the door, please?"

She did.

"I owe you an apology," he said.

"No . . ."

"I think maybe I had the wrong impression of what you wanted out of this job. I think our relationship might have clouded my judgment."

Lucinda thought this was awfully mature of him, all things considered, so she said, "Thank you."

"And I also think if you're really serious about this, as a career, then maybe this isn't the right thing for both of us."

"Maybe what isn't the right thing?"

"Lucinda. Please don't play dumb."

"I'm not playing dumb," said Lucinda. "I'm being dumb. Are you breaking up with me? Or firing me?"

And Gavin laughed and said, "Oh God, no!"

Lucinda relaxed a little and said, "Oh, okay."

"You're not fired, no. This is just a breakup."

Lucinda quickly unrelaxed the little she had just relaxed and shouted, "What?!"

"Please don't make a scene," said Gavin. "I'm doing this because I care about you."

"You're breaking up with me, at work? Who does that?"

But Lucinda knew who does that. The kind of person who doesn't want the woman he's breaking up with to make a scene does that.

"This doesn't have to be ugly. The truth is neither of us ever really understood what the other one was looking for."

Lucinda nodded, and went back to her office, and thought about how incredible it was that in one conversation Gavin could break up with her, and also not give her a promotion, and also say, "I owe you an apology," all without actually apologizing.

But now, Lucinda was getting very good at not thinking about any of that. In fact, that night, she had trouble sleeping, because she was so consumed by not thinking.

Lucinda woke up and it was Friday, and she couldn't believe how long it had taken to get her to Friday. Every day had felt incredibly long and yet also incredibly empty. The week had been an endless string of moments, each one packed, stuffed, overflowing with emptiness.

At the end of the day, Debbie spilled into Lucinda's doorway.

"Can I get you dinner?" she asked.

"Not tonight, thanks. I'm heading out soon."

Debbie glanced up and down the hallway and then leaned farther into Lucinda's office. "Hey, can I talk to you? About the Cinnamon Sugar Blast Oat Cubes?"

And Lucinda said, "You know, I was hoping you would."

"I guess that must have seemed pretty random. The truth is I wanted to just get you a watch, but Kelly checks the receipts and I thought that would look bad, but I figured Cinnamon Sugar Blast Oat Cubes is a food item, so technically it's okay."

Lucinda looked at the picture of the free Minions wristwatch on the front of the box. "Why did you want to get me a watch, Debbie?"

"Well, sometimes I look at you when I'm walking by your office to Conference Room H, and—"

"You look at me?"

"No, not like in a creepy way—I just mean I see you."

"Okay."

"And I see you check your phone a lot, and every time you do, you make this angry face. I feel so bad, it makes me want to come in and give you a hug—and I know that's inappropriate, but I thought: Maybe if I got her a watch, she wouldn't have to check her phone so much."

Lucinda looked back at the box, then back at Debbie. She thought about how pure Debbie was, how young and unsullied. She thought about how sad it was that one day Debbie would fall in love with someone who would at first appreciate all that was special about her, but eventually learn how to take her for granted. She thought about how this person didn't deserve Debbie, this person who didn't know how rare it was to be loved by a person so tender.

"You know, you're a lot better than the last receptionist we had."

Debbie blushed. "Oh, I'm just doing the best I can. Every morning, I remind myself: Debbie, you're doing the best you can, and that's all that you can do, and that's enough!"

Lucinda realized this was maybe the longest conversation the two had ever shared. "I'm going to miss you around here when you ship off to law school," she said. "Where are you applying?"

Debbie laughed. "Oh God, no, I'm not— No. I could never get into law school. I'm just happy to help out at a place like this. I think the work the guys do here is so important and good."

"Just the guys?"

"I'm sorry. The women too. I didn't mean any offense."

Lucinda smiled. "I think you'd actually be a good lawyer. You're very observant. You should take the LSAT."

"I have," said Debbie. "Three times."

"Oh."

"It's okay," said Debbie. "You know, I used to be super-bummed, but the truth is you can get over anything with enough time. That was the other part of the idea behind the watch, the first part being the thing about you not having to look at your phone. The other part was so that you could remember that time was passing. For most things, really, the only thing to do is just let there be time."

"Well, thanks again," said Lucinda.

Debbie nodded. "You know, I always thought I would be a lawyer, but I kind of live my life by the law of: Hey, if it's not meant to be . . . you know?"

"Yeah," said Lucinda. "I feel like I once wrote a memo on that law."

Debbie laughed. "You're really funny."

Okay, Lucinda thought: So I'm funny.

No, she thought: I'm *really* funny. I am above-average funny.

On Monday, Gavin swung by Lucinda's office to ask how she was doing on that memo about whether a ferret could be classified as a service animal in Colorado.

And Lucinda said, "I'm doing fine, thanks."

And the truth was she *was* doing fine, which in the scheme of things was not as good as good, but loads better than bad.

"I like your watch," said Gavin. "Minions."

"Yeah," said Lucinda. "Minions."

She returned her gaze to the computer screen and got back to work.

More of the You
That You Already
Are

Being a president of the United States is the easiest thing in the world basically. The main thing is you gotta show up on time. I know this because one time I show up like three minutes late, which is still technically on time basically, and Mr. Gupta just about bites my head off.

Six fifteen means six fifteen, he's like.

And I'm like, I'm sorry, the traffic—which isn't even the real reason I'm late, but that's just what I say now, because one time when I was late at this Quiznos I worked at, I told my boss it was because of Ramona, and at first he was real nice about it, but I could tell it bummed him out, and then like a week later I got fired because he said my "family situation" was interfering with my "job performance," which wasn't even true really, because I could still make a killer sub like nobody's business, but anyway now when I'm late I just say it's because of traffic.

So then Mr. Gupta's like, If you can't make it a priority to be here on time, I'm sure I can find someone who will.

And I want to be like, Come on, man, I'm like three minutes late, but then I know he'd be like, And look at all this additional time we're wasting arguing about it. And, sure, then I could be like, Yeah, but no one is forcing you to argue with me, you could just let it slide—but the main thing you gotta know about Mr. Gupta is that Mr. Gupta is never going to let anything slide, so you're better off usually just cutting your losses, which I guess is also one of the things you gotta know if you want to be a president.

So instead I'm just like, I'm very sorry, sir. It won't happen again.

So then you go see Emika at Wardrobe to pick up your costume. You're supposed to show Emika your park ID with your picture and your presidential number on it, so she knows what suit to pull, but if you've been there more than like a day, Emika knows who you are and she's getting your costume before you've even pulled out your wallet.

You walk into the room and Emika lights up and is like, Well, if it isn't President Arthur! Technically she's not supposed to say that, because according to park policy you're not really President Arthur until you put the costume on. Park policy is very specific on this point—I guess because one time Thomas Jefferson was going around town all like, I'm Thomas Jefferson, and trying to get free shit out of it, like milkshakes or whatever, and picking up girls, and when that got back to park management, Mr. Gupta got his ass chewed out by the guys at corporate, so then we all got our asses chewed out by Mr. Gupta.

Anyway, Emika's real friendly and she's got great stories even though they're never really about anything. I guess it's more the way she tells the stories. Like the story could be: Teddy Roosevelt lost a button and Emika had to sew on a new one—but from the way she tells it you'd think it was the most interesting story in the world, full of twists and turns and heroes and villains. One time Valerie took a double shift, because I guess Emika had to go to a wedding, and when I walked into Wardrobe and saw Valerie in the morning, that was probably the worst day of my life. Also, that was the day the doctor told us Ramona's sickness had spread to her bones, so it was definitely a real bad day. I'm not saying the two things are related necessarily, Valerie sitting in for Emika and my sister's sickness spreading to her bones; all I know is I feel much better every morning when Emika's there. Nothing against Valerie—I just like Emika better.

Anyway, after you get your costume from Emika, you go into the changing room and put your big giant head on, and then—ta-da!—you're a president. Being Chester A. Arthur is like the easiest president to be, because basically you just have to stand around outside the entrance to the Rutherford B. Hedge Maze by the Bridge to a Better Tomorrow over the River of Racial Intolerance, and sometimes Lincoln walks by, and then people ask if you'll take their picture with Lincoln, and you're just like: Sure, I'm Chester A. Arthur, I'm not doing anything.

And okay, some days it feels like, what's even the point of being a president if you're just going to be Chester A. Arthur? Like, there's this other guy who started on the same day I did and he gets to be Franklin Roosevelt, which is a doubly sweet gig, because first of all, everyone loves FDR, but the even sweeter part is you get to sit down all day, except for during the *1600 Pennsylvania Avenue Revue,* when at the end of your New Deal song, you stand up for like five seconds, and it's a *huge fucking to-do.* You get a round of applause just for standing up, and you don't even have to do a softshoe routine like Calvin Coolidge does. But also, if you're FDR, the shitty part is you gotta memorize all these facts about FDR, who was president for like a hundred years just about, and people are always coming up to you, asking questions like "What's the only thing we have to fear?" and "What do you have against the Japanese anyway?" and if you get them even a little bit wrong, then some kid's jerk parent is going to complain to park management, and then you know Mr. Gupta is going to get all up in your ass about it, so all things being equal, I'd rather be Chester A. Arthur, honestly.

Some days Benjamin Harrison wanders by for a couple hours, which isn't so bad, because at least it's someone to talk to. Benjamin Harrison is an all right guy, so long as you don't get on the subject of this extra-large fuck-doll he got on the internet. You would think that would be a real easy topic to avoid, because how often do extra-large fuck-dolls come up in everyday conversation? But Harrison spent like eight hundred bucks on this thing, and I guess the more money you spend on something the more you want to talk about it, even if the thing is a big silicon woman that you have sex with.

He's like, Normally these things go for thousands of dollars, but I got mine cheap because I got it used.

And I'm just like, Cool, man.

And he's like, Some people think it's weird. But I don't think it's weird. It's just masturbating. Everybody does it.

And I'm just like, Yep.

And he's like, If I told you that you could have the best orgasm of your life for eight hundred dollars, wouldn't you take that deal?

This question is totally bonkers to me, because I can't even picture having all of eight hundred dollars at one time, just lying around, waiting for me to do something with it. Like, could you imagine being like: Hmm, what should I do with this Almost a Thousand Dollars? I guess I could use it to pay for half a month of rent on this shitty apartment I share with my mom and my sister, or maybe I could find a pretty lady and take her out for a real dinner, like to a place with cloth napkins and everything. Or how about I upgrade to a better cable package, with like those fancy movie stations, so Ramona doesn't have to watch junky talk shows all day? Oh, wait!

I know! Why don't I go online and see if I can't find a fake plastic woman for me to jack myself off into?

I don't even know where I'd keep one of those things. Like, do you also have to buy a special closet for it? I don't have space for that shit. Harrison keeps his in the back of his van, but I guess if you're me, you just keep it in the living room?

I'm sure Ramona would get a kick out of it. She'd give it a name, like Noreen or some shit, and when I got home from work, she'd go, Your new girlfriend Noreen and I had the grandest of days together. Did you know Noreen was a child tennis phenom before her stroke left her completely immobile? Fascinating woman. Elegant lady.

And then Mom would pull me aside and say, You have to get rid of that thing. Ramona spent the whole day talking to it. She asked me to make it a cup of tea.

And then I'd take it back to my bedroom and try to have sex with it, but instead I'd keep thinking about how sad it was that she was a child tennis phenom who'd had a stroke. So, all things considered, it's probably better I don't get the extra-large fuck-doll.

But Benjamin Harrison isn't a bad guy ninety percent of the time. And sometimes he has interesting things to talk about, like one time, he saw the new X-Men movie, and then on Monday, he told me the whole story, so I didn't have to pay to see it myself. That was pretty decent of him, and he didn't have to do that. He even acted out some of the fight scenes. He also always has good gossip about what's been going on around the park, on account of him being a floater and all, so sometimes he can tell you shit like: a little kid peed all over James Monroe. That's hilarious, because first of all, if you knew James Monroe even a little bit, you'd be like: Fuck that guy. But also because second of all, Founding Fathers Square is about as far as you can get from Wardrobe, so you have to imagine Monroe having to walk all the way across the park covered in little kid piss, and just picturing that could be the highlight of your week pretty much.

So whenever Harrison wants to talk about his extra-large fuck-doll that he keeps in the back of his van, and I want to be like, Dude, shut the fuck up, nobody cares, instead I'm just like, Come on, man, there are kids here. And that usually does the trick.

If any guest at the park wants to talk to you, which basically only happens if there's a long line to talk to one of the important presidents, there's really just two things you have to know about Chester A. Arthur: one, I became president when President Garfield pissed somebody off and got assassinated, and two, my primary achievement was the Pendleton Reform Act. Then, if someone asks you what the Pendleton Reform Act was, you can probably jump off the ground and fly to Hollywood and kiss a supermodel on the mouth, because you are definitely in a dream right now, because literally no one ever asks a follow-up question about the Pendleton Reform Act.

Then at the end of the day, you change out of your costume, and you return it to Valerie in Wardrobe, or sometimes Emika, if Valerie and Emika switched shifts. I like seeing Emika in the morning, because then it feels like it's going to be a good, normal day, with no surprises, but if Emika and Valerie switch shifts and I see Emika at the end of the day, that's not the worst thing in the world either I guess. The only problem is I feel bad giving my sweaty costume to Emika for her to clean, which is I guess the downside of Emika working the night shift. I like to imagine Emika coming in to work in the morning and pulling my costume out of the dryer, clean and warm, maybe even holding her cheek up to Chester A. Arthur's chest, to get a little of that warmth.

Anyway, that's like a typical day, or it was before all this shit started going down. The shit starts on a Sunday, of course. Shit always starts on a Sunday, I guess because that's our last day, so if management wants to flip some switch that makes everything go all bat-ass nutty, everyone can cool off over "the weekend," which is what we call Monday, and then when we come back in to work on Tuesday it's like nothing ever happened.

Anyway, I'm already in a bad way (on the day the shit starts going down), because the night before Ramona gets a bad reaction to her new medication, so I'm up all night, keeping her company while she throws up every twenty minutes. We try to make a game of it, where every time she barfs, I ask her a question about one of her favorite things.

Hey, Ramona, what do you think of the new Drake album?

BARF.

Really? You used to love Drake. You don't like the new stuff?

BARF.

Wow. Strong reaction. Guess I should delete all the Drake songs off your phone. Guess you hate Drake now.

And Ramona smiles, even while barfing, and is like, You're so stupid.

And I'm glad I could be there for Ramona and make her smile, but the end result is I'm real tired at work the next day, which is not the way you want to be when shit starts to go down.

At this point, Van Buren's been on leave for about a week, on account of him taking his wiener out and waving it at a bunch of deaf kids during the fireworks show. It's not that he's a pervert, he tried to explain; he just got confused between deaf kids and blind kids. I guess Mr. Gupta didn't go for that explanation, because after a week, word trickles down that Van Buren's not coming back. And not just that Van Buren, Harrison says, any Van Buren.

I don't get it. I'm like, What, are we just not going to have a Van Buren?

And Harrison's like, Would you miss him?

Next thing is, Mr. Gupta's calling an all-presidents meeting, after hours. This is serious business, an all-presidents meeting. Mostly, news goes out in small groups, and by the time they call in my group (my group is Group 5), word's already spread anyway. Last time I can remember an all-presidents meeting was when Madison was racist to one of the guests, so Mr. Gupta called us in all at once so he could tell us: Don't be racist. And Madison's like, But what if your guy really was racist? Like, what if he owned slaves? And Mr. Gupta's like, Yeah, okay, but still: don't be racist.

This time the meeting's about Van Buren.

I'm sure you're all wondering why Van Buren isn't here, Mr. Gupta's like.

And Franklin Pierce is like, Because he showed his wiener to those deaf kids.

And Mr. Gupta gets all flustered and is like, No—well, yes, but that's—

He takes a moment to regain his composure.

I'm sure you're all wondering why Thomas Jefferson isn't here, Mr. Gupta's like.

I look around. I hadn't noticed, but sure enough Jefferson isn't there. In fact, a lot of people aren't there.

Mr. Gupta smiles and is all, I'm sure you're thinking, How are we going to open the park next week without Andrew Jackson, or James Monroe, or John Adams, or even . . . George Washington?!

I look around. Yeah, pretty weird.

Well, Mr. Gupta continues, what if I told you we could get ten presidents for the manpower of one? And not just people pretending to be presidents—real actual presidents?

Just then, the door to the Extra Office Where No One's Allowed opens and a white lady in a suit backs out into the bullpen holding a long chain. And she calls into the extra office like, Come on. Come on, buddy.

A low groan comes out of the Extra Office Where No One's Allowed, and Benjamin Harrison and I look at each other, like, *Well, this is some shit, huh?*

The white lady looks at us and smiles, white-lady-ly, and is just like, He's very shy.

And Mr. Gupta is all annoyed now, like he called this whole meeting and everything and now whatever is back there on the other side of that chain—which I guess was the whole point of it—won't even come out. And he's just like, Is he coming or not?

And the lady ignores Mr. Gupta and just keeps looking into the room and is like, Come on, buddy.

And the low groan gets louder and out comes this . . . thing on a leash—a terrifying ten-foot-tall behemoth of a man, heaving with every breath, eyes bulging, lower jaw jutted, a gnarly rag doll made of people, stuffed into a half-buttoned colonial outfit. And the room fills with gasps and OhMyGod!!s and WhatTheShit?!?!s, and the lady speaks over us and announces, Please do not alarm him. He is very temperamental.

And Mr. Gupta shouts out, Quiet? Everyone will be quiet, please, for our guest?

And Kennedy's like, Er, ahh, what the hell is that thing?

And the lady's like, It's not a what-is-that-thing, it's a who-is-that-thing.

Mr. Gupta beams: You know, a lot of you have maybe forgotten how important Presidentland is. A lot of you think maybe this is all fun and games. But actually, Presidentland is a very educational place for families. A lot of respectable people think what we do here is very noble work.

I look over at the large man-thing. It's drooling and looking around like it's scanning the room for an exit.

I work for Frank Fielding, says the white lady.

And everyone just kind of looks at her, like, *Who?*

And she says again, annoyed: Frank Fielding? The Frank and Felicity Fielding Foundation? Funding tomorrow's solutions today for yesterday's problems tomorrow?

And I'm like, Oh yeah, 'cause I'm pretty sure I heard that in a commercial once.

The lady is smiling super-wide now: Frank Fielding is a true visionary and a game changer. Some people say he's like the new Steve Jobs, but I actually think he's more like Che Guevara meets Gandhi—if Che Guevara and Gandhi were billionaires.

And Harding's like, It kind of sounds like you got a crush on Frank Fielding.

And the lady's like, I do not have a crush on him, because he is my boss, and besides he has a wife so that is impossible.

Please ignore President Harding, Mr. Gupta coughs out; he is very rude.

The lady continues: We at the Frank and Felicity Fielding Foundation think what you do here is so vital and necessary. After all, who are presidents if not the innovators and disrupters of history?

And Hoover shouts out, Who indeed? and Hoover's idiot buddies start giggling, and Mr. Gupta's like, Guys, please.

The lady continues: But why remember what history *was*, when instead you can experience what history *is*? Through samples from their distant progeny, we at the FieldingCorp Research Labs were able to reconstruct with eighty-eight percent accuracy literally up to twelve percent of the actual genetic makeup of the fathers of this nation. With that DNA data, and the world's most powerful 4-D printers, we were able to construct our tax-deductible gift to the park—Waj'm Maj'vht. Say hello, Waj'm!

She yanks on the chain and the beast groans a plaintive, guttural wail.

Waj'm Maj'vht is a perfect genetic combination of the first ten presidents, Mr. Gupta announces proudly.

WAJ'M MAJ'VHT! the lady repeats. Washington! Adams! Jefferson! . . . The rest!

And Mr. Gupta continues: Not just guys in costumes, I'm saying—this guy is the actual presidents Oh no he is vomiting.

Sure enough this thing is now puking all over the floor—like for real just fire-hosing chunks all over the place. And part of me wants to cut through the awkwardness by asking the monster what it thinks of the new Drake album, but I know I probably shouldn't in front of the white lady.

She starts stroking his scraggly hair and says, It's okay. This is natural. People do this, Waj'm. This is natural.

And Mr. Gupta's like, Please ignore the vomiting. Once we get the vomiting under control, Waj'm Maj'vht will be beloved by children and visitors to the park of all ages!

And that's the end of the meeting.

Tuesday morning, I ask Emika at Wardrobe if she's seen the new addition to the park.

Seen it, she's like. Who do you think made the costume for it?

I immediately feel stupid for asking. Of course Emika would know all about it, what with Wardrobe being so close to Mr. Gupta's office and right next to the Extra Office Where No One's Allowed.

She zips up the back of my suit and I'm like, What do you make of it?

I think it's kind of neat, she shrugs. Science and all.

And I'm just like, Yeah, I get that part of it—and I definitely do get that part of it—but I guess from where I'm sitting it's like, maybe ease up a little, Science. You know? It's like, where's the fire, Science?

And she's like, Yeah, no, I get that too. I like the eyes, though.

The eyes?

Waj'm's eyes? Did you see them?

And I have to confess I did not spend a lot of time looking into the eyes of the puking monster.

They're soulful, she's like. Those eyes have seen a lot. Ten presidents, right?

And I'm like, That's what they say.

And Emika gets all thoughtful: Ten men in one body—I feel like there's a lot going on in there—I mean, when he's not vomiting.

And I'm just like, I guess it takes all kinds.

And she gives me a quirky little smile and says, Guess so.

If there's a thing I like about Emika it's that she sees stuff kind of crooked like that. Like to say that Waj'm Maj'vht isn't just a monster but ten men in one body with real soulful eyes. It's funny, but also kind of sweet. I don't really get the science of it, so I don't know if that's how it actually is or not, but like I said, it's an interesting way to look at it.

Benjamin Harrison swings by my post after lunch and I tell him what Emika said, about Waj'm being ten men and all, and Harrison thinks that's pretty hilarious.

Look, man, he says, I spent all morning at Founding Fathers Square, and let me tell you, that dude is barely doing the work of one man.

And I'm like, No?

And he's like, Dude's tied to a pole like a tetherball. He mostly just sits there, jabbing the ground with a rock. Every once in a while, he blurts out a phrase, like "the insurmountable folly of intransigence," but mostly he just kind of grunts and falls down.

And I'm like, Sounds like those scientists maybe got a little too much James Monroe in there.

And Harrison's like, Haha.

Meanwhile, Ramona needs to go to the clinic to get the results of her blood work, and Mom wants me to come with, in case the news is bad. It's on a Thursday of course, which is the worst time to miss work, on account of Thursday's a big day for field trips.

I try to tell Mom, Things are weird over there. It's not a good time to ask for time off.

And she's just like, I'm sorry your sister picked a bad time to get sick; that was real selfish of her, huh?

And I'm like, Why do I gotta go? If the news is bad, what difference does it make?

And Mom is like, Ramona needs to know that you're there for her.

And I'm like, I'm there for her by going to the job that pays for our rent and covers her medical costs.

And Mom is like, Will you just ask?

So then like an idiot, I'm sitting outside Mr. Gupta's office end-of-day Wednesday, waiting for him to finish up whatever meeting he's in. I'm sitting in one of those dinky chairs he's got in the waiting area right outside and I'm hearing him shout through the walls: People are asking, Where's Washington? Where's Andrew Jackson? And they are not happy with your . . . confounding simulacrum.

And I hear the white lady say, Okay, I acknowledge your feedback and I am internalizing it. What I'm hearing is we were too bold with our pilot program. Obviously, we're putting too much pressure on one hybrid to try to capture the magic of guys like Washington and Jackson and what have you.

And Mr. Gupta's like, I mean, those are some of our most popular guys.

Well, what if you hired back the original ten and we gave you a new hybrid? One who replaced your *least* popular guys? That's low risk for you, and it gives us the chance to work out the kinks.

And Mr. Gupta's like, Honestly I've soured on this whole cloning ten presidents at once idea. Maybe we should just stick with the people in costumes.

And the white lady's like, Mr. Gupta, I am very surprised and disappointed to hear you say that. Do you not remember the agreement your bosses signed with FieldingCorp, giving us an ownership stake in the park so we could beta test new biotechnologies? I would hate to take you to court over this, especially because everyone at the foundation still believes so passionately in the mission of Presidentland and the potential of our work to make history come alive.

And Mr. Gupta's like, Please, no one needs to go to court.

And the lady's like, I completely agree. So, we're definitely on the same page there. Plus, we're on the same page as far as the Waj'm rollout being unfortunately premature. We all got a little excited, which is not a crime. This is why we try things. We need to allow ourselves to fail, so that we can fail upward. We'll try again with different presidents, yes?

And Mr. Gupta's like, We can try.

And the lady's like, Lower-status presidents?

And Mr. Gupta's like, Yes.

And the lady's like, Marvelous. I knew you could be reasonable.

Well, I might not be the sharpest commemorative butter knife in the presidential gift shop but I'm not a complete moron, so I know this isn't great news for old Chester A. Arthur.

I duck across the hall into Wardrobe, where Harrison is still getting out of his costume. I tell him the whole thing, and he's like, Well, we're fucked.

And I'm like, No. Yeah?

And he's like, Look, man, I'm Benjamin Harrison—the less famous Harrison. Think about that for a second, I'm less notable than the guy who was only president for a month. And you're Chester A. Arthur. Your primary achievement was like the Peabody Referendum or some bullshit.

And I'm like, Pendleton Reform Act.

Who gives a shit? We're bottom ten, easy, any way you measure it. If they're getting rid of ten presidents, you're a goner. I'm a goner.

When I get back home and Mom asks me what happened with the asking for the time off, I just say it's a no-go.

And she's like, What the hell does that mean, it's a no-go?

And I'm like, Sometimes things are no-gos, Mom.

So now I'm figuring my days at the park are numbered. Don't get me wrong, this is a true bummer, because we for real need the money right now, but I'm not thinking I'll miss the park itself much. I certainly won't miss all the dipwad presidents who work here.

When I was a kid, I used to come to Presidentland and dream of being a president one day—like that's how small and stupid my imagination was, I thought dressing up in a big suit and putting on a big foam head and acting all fancy at a theme park was like the height of importance and sophistication. The truth is the whole place is just a bunch of assholes, and it turns out making an asshole a president just means you end up with an asshole president. Probably could've guessed that—being president doesn't change you, not really; it just brings out more of the you that you already are.

But I will miss Emika in Wardrobe, and maybe the idea of not seeing her every day is getting me sentimental or maybe all that time in the suit in the hot sun is making me stupid or maybe since I'm probably going to get canned soon I just don't give a shit anymore in any direction, but whatever the reason, I decide to ask Emika if she wants to get a drink sometime after work.

As soon as I ask her, I regret it, because first of all, of course she doesn't, and second of all, where am I going to take her? The only bar I ever go to is the one in the back of the bowling alley, and you can't really take a girl there, because it's full of weird old guys who are all trying to sell you hand soap, on account of this pyramid scheme that took certain pockets of the town by storm last year. I feel like if I tried to take Emika to a nice bar—like a wine bar or an upscale club or something—the bouncer would take one look at me and be like, Are you kidding me? And Emika would look at me and be like, You know, I didn't see it before, but now that I think about it, this bouncer's got a point, as far as the "Are you kidding me?" part.

But then I forget all of that, because Emika says: I'd love to.

So now I'm thinking: Fuck the Pendleton Reform Act, because Chester A. Arthur's new primary achievement is getting Emika from Wardrobe to get a drink with him sometime after work.

For the whole week pretty much I'm floating on air. Like even when Mom tells me the results from the clinic aren't so good, I can't help but be an optimist about it. I go into Ramona's room and I sit on the side of her bed, and I'm like, Clinics. What do they know, right?

And Ramona laughs, and coughs, and is like, Total quacks. I told Mom, no more medical advice from people who take seven years to graduate college.

Yeah, I'm like, Bunch of slowpokes! Myself, I'm a cynic, when it comes to clinics.

Clinic cynic, Ramona rasps, and I can tell she's getting tired, so I say one more thing, which is: Hey, the main thing is it's gonna be okay.

And she closes her eyes and says, Yeah. It's gonna be okay.

Well, meanwhile, the date with Emika goes south before it even begins. And of course it does, because why did I think I ever deserved a thing to happen to me that was just wholly good?

Look, she's like, just as we're sitting down. I need to say something right off the bat. I don't know why you asked me for drinks, and I don't want to be presumptuous, but I think I should tell you, I'm kind of in love with someone.

And I'm like, Oh, cool, no, that's no problem. The someone you're in love with is me, right?

And she looks all uncomfortable and is like, No, sorry.

And I'm like, No, I got it, I was just making a joke.

And she looks even *more* all uncomfortable and is like, Oh, cool joke.

And I'm like, Well, this is going great.

And she's like, I really do like you as a friend, though, and I was stoked you wanted to spend more time with me.

And I'm like, Well, good news is things won't be awkward for you at work after this, on account of I'm probably getting fired soon.

And she's like, Why do you figure that?

I tell her what I heard, about how Mr. Gupta and the white lady are going to bring back the first ten guys and replace ten other presidents with a new mega-president, and what Harrison said about us both being doomed.

And Emika goes, But you can't lump yourself in with Benjamin Harrison. Of course Mr. Gupta would want to get rid of him; that guy's a dirtbag. He's always looking at my boobs from inside his big giant president head.

How can you tell?

Because the whole head tilts down.

Why doesn't he just look with his eyes?

I don't know! He's an idiot. But what I'm saying is you're not like that. You're a hard worker and you've got a good attitude mostly, which actually sets you apart from a lot of the other guys here. If it's my opinion, I think you should fight for it.

But here I'm like, What's to fight for? If he's going to replace the bottom ten guys, either that's me or it's not. There's nothing I can do.

And Emika's like, Hold up, did you say bottom ten guys?

And I'm like, Yeah . . .

Emika thinks for a second, then leans in close. Listen, she's like. I've been spending some time in the Extra Office Where No One's Allowed . . .

And I'm like, No shit?

And she's like, I know technically I'm not allowed in there—no one is—but I'm usually the first person at the park, other than Amir from Security, and it's so peaceful in there . . .

And I'm all, Isn't that where the big guy lives?

And she goes, I could probably get in trouble just for talking about it. But my point is the white lady has kind of made it her office, and so she and Mr. Gupta have a lot of conversations in there.

What kind of conversations?

Well, I don't know. Like I said, I just go in there early in the morning, and then I leave before anyone else shows up. But they've got a big whiteboard in there with all the presidents' names on it, and they keep rearranging it, putting them in different orders.

What's the order based on?

I don't know, but Washington and Lincoln are always right at the top, one and two. And the bottom keeps changing, but it's usually like Hayes, Pierce, Fillmore, that kind of thing.

And me? Chester Arthur?

Emika frowns and then says, Like I said, it keeps changing.

So it's not set in stone who the bottom guys are—it's not like based on historical importance?

Honestly, if I had to guess I'd say it was based on merch sales.

And so then I'm thinking that's fucked-up, because I just don't have that much merch to move. But then another part of me is like: Well, there's a chance.

So on the bus ride home, I'm doing the math in my head, like, Okay, who's definitely staying? Definitely all the recent presidents—everyone back to Franklin Roosevelt if I'm being honest—because old-timers love getting their pictures taken with presidents they've lived through. And the first ten—there's no way they'd bring them all back just to fire them again. So, that's already twenty-four people who are almost definitely not getting fired, and I haven't even gotten to Lincoln yet.

I start to freak out, but then I realize that between Tyler and FDR, pretty much the only sure bets are Lincoln and Teddy Roosevelt.

Then there are guys like Grant and Coolidge—not guaranteed to stay, but definitely more likely than me—and if we're really being rigorous, we can probably throw Wilson in that category too. Hoover and Buchanan might squeak in, just on account of how bad they were, and people love hearing about how Garfield and McKinley got shot.

So that leaves only eleven presidents, including me. Could I be a bigger draw than ten of them? I make a list and I run through them over and over:

Polk

Taylor

Fillmore

Pierce

A. Johnson

Hayes

Cleveland

B. Harrison

Taft

Harding

These are the guys I've gotta beat. Tough, but definitely doable. Most of them probably don't even realize they're on the chopping block, and if any of them do, they might figure—like Harrison did— well, what's the point in trying if I'm already getting sacked?

Next day, I show up on time and ready to work. From my angle on things, I'm thinking I need a three-pronged approach here.

The first prong is all about projecting an air of professionalism and respect in front of Mr. Gupta. Good morning, Mr. Gupta, I'm like. It's a beautiful day to educate our guests about presidential history, I'm like.

The second prong is about driving up interest in Chester A.

Arthur with park visitors. There's only so much I can do on this front, because most people aren't starting their day thinking, Boy, I can't wait to meet Chet Arthur and possibly buy some Chet Arthur–related merchandise. But the truth is I can leverage what I know about how the park functions to my advantage here. Like, for example, Teddy Roosevelt is always complaining that he gets slammed in the afternoons, right around one, because that's when mini-Rushmore opens, but Lincoln doesn't show up until after the Emancipation Celebration, and now that Washington and Jefferson have been replaced by a barely sentient drooling man-wall who needs to remain tied to his post—for the safety of the children— well, it creates a lot of work for Teddy Roosevelt.

Roosevelt already sort of likes me, as it happens, because one time he saw me riding my bike to work before it got stolen, and then for like a week, whenever he saw me on the other side of the Bridge to a Better Tomorrow, he would shout, Hey! Bike! And I'd be like, Yeah! You said it!

So it isn't hard to start a conversation with him now where I'm like, Hey, man, I think I can help with your one o'clock crunch. I'm barely doing anything at one—like my area completely empties out—so if you send people my way, I can totally handle them.

And he's like, Sure, but how am I gonna do that?

Here's what you gotta do. You gotta tell people: Used to be, only way to get ahead in politics was through crooked dealings. Myself, I'm a mad respectable individual, but I never would have been president if not for the Pendleton Reform Act. And when people say, What's the Pendleton Reform Act? you say: Why don't you go ask Chester A. Arthur?

And he's like, Is that true? About me not being president if not for the whatever whatever act you just said?

And I'm like, Look, man, there's no way to know for sure what would have happened without the Pendleton Reform Act—time is a many-forked river that flows in one direction only—but we do know that there was a reform act passed, and then years later you became president. I don't think it's a stretch to say those two things are definitely related.

And he's like, All right, well, at this point, I'll try anything.

Great. So say all that, and then if people are still on the fence, you can say: Perhaps no one changed the course of U.S. presidential history more than Chester A. Arthur.

And he's like, Yeah, I'm not going to say that.

And I'm like, Yeah, that part's too much, but the rest of it?

And he's like, Yeah, the rest of it, fine.

The third prong of my plan—and this is the prong I feel not so hot about—is throwing some of those other guys under the bus. We have these anonymous Ask Not What Your Country Can Do for You cards that we're supposed to fill out to report other employees when we witness violations of park policy. Everyone treats them like a big joke, but the truth is there are a lot of violations that happen every day. Like, for example, everyone knows Hayes is vaping in the park, even though the park has a strict no vaping policy. I fill out an Ask Not What Your Country Can Do for You card about Hayes vaping, and that night, Mr. Gupta calls him into his office.

I feel gross about this on the one hand, because like is Hayes really hurting anybody by sneaking vapes? And is Pierce really hurting anyone through his repeated Use of Anachronistic References, which I also write a card about? Or what about Fillmore letting three kids go at once on Fillmore's Flume, even though Fillmore's Flume is expressly designed to be enjoyed by two Friends of Fillmore at a time? But on the other hand, park policy is clear, and it's every man for himself out there, and I'm not just looking out for me at this point—I've got people depending on me—and if other presidents are going to leave themselves vulnerable by making stupid mistakes, then maybe they don't deserve to be presidents in the first place.

The one guy I don't write up is Benjamin Harrison, even though he definitely breaks park policy all the time, like when I see him talk to guests about his sword collection, and it's unclear if actual Benjamin Harrison had a sword collection or if he's just talking about himself. But he's always been regular decent to me, and I feel like loyalty has to be good for something in this cutthroat world, because otherwise what are we even doing?

So like after a week of my three-pronged approach, Mr. Gupta calls me into his office. I've been really impressed by how you've been performing lately, he's like.

And I'm like, Just doing my job.

And he's like, The guys at corporate are really impressed too. There's been an uptick in sales of Arthur merch. I want you to know that the right people are noticing.

And I'm like, That's really great to hear, sir.

You treat me with respect, he's like. You treat this job with respect. Not everybody does that.

And I'm like, No?

He's like, I know everyone wants to have a good time, but this is a job, and people need to recognize that.

Oh totally. That's always been my thing, one hundred percent, it being a job and all.

It's not like I like being the bad guy, he goes. I know everyone thinks I'm a hard-ass, but I'm getting pressure from all sides, you know?

And I go, Yeah, I know what you mean.

And he goes, Okay, well, keep it up.

On the bus ride home I think about Mr. Gupta for the first time not just as a boss, but also as a person who exists and has feelings. I wonder if when he was hired to run the park, he realized what a bunch of assholes all the presidents were going to be. I know that by doing a good job I'm making his life easier—and even though making Mr. Gupta's life easier is not *why* I do a good job, I'm not mad at that part of it. It also feels nice to know that my efforts have been noticed, because so much of the time the lesson of life is that everything's built on bullshit and nothing you do matters. It's cool to feel like I have some control over my own destiny for once, especially because Ramona's condition has taken a turn for the worse and she has to spend a couple days in the hospital, for observation and possibly another surgery.

The next day I feel motivated to go in early, just to keep up my streak of going above and beyond—and also because without Ramona in the apartment, it turns out my apartment is a real bummer. I catch the first bus before it even gets light out, and when I show up at the park, the only people there are Amir in Security and Emika.

You're here early, she's like.

And I'm like, Yeah, sorry. I know you like to be alone in the mornings.

And she's like, This is perfect actually, because I want you to meet someone. Remember when I told you I was in love?

And now I'm really regretting coming in early, because I can already tell this is going to be a whole thing.

She takes me to the Extra Office Where No One's Allowed, and I'm like, Emika, I'm pretty sure we're not supposed to be back here.

And she's like, It's fine, no one will know; I do this every day.

In the corner, chained to a wall, is Waj'm Maj'vht, glaring menacingly, breathing heavily.

Hi, baby, Emika's like, and Waj'm Maj'vht continues to do his thing, which is sitting on the ground, chained to the wall, glaring menacingly and breathing heavily.

I'm like, This is the guy you're in love with?

Emika smiles. You see it, right?

Waj'm grunts: Prolonged conflagration . . . self-evident . . . Abigail!

He curls into a squat and starts whittling a stick.

And I'm like, Don't take this the wrong way, and I'm not always the best judge of character, but he kind of seems like a wild monster.

He's not a monster! I love him. I feed him whole onions that he eats like an apple.

And now I'm thinking, If this is the kind of guy Emika is into, then I really never stood a chance with her.

And Emika's like, I know it's hard to understand. I was afraid of him at first too, but he's really a gentle soul, and he has the heart of ten men. Isn't that right, Waj'm?

Waj'm looks up at us and grunts: Abuse of liberty is the bone and sinew, *Abigail*!

Emika goes, That's right, Waj'm.

And I go, You know, we're really not supposed to be in this room. We could get in big trouble.

And for some reason, Emika starts crying and is like, He knows he doesn't belong here, but it's not his fault he exists. He's not the one who made him in a lab.

And the most fucked-up part is now I love Emika more than ever, seeing how worked up she gets over this other guy, who isn't even really a guy, hardly, as much as a weird deformed historical mishmash. I want to hold her and stroke her hair and tell her everything's going to be okay, but we are at work, after all, and the park staff behavioral guidelines are very clear on appropriate and inappropriate touch ever since Eisenhower goosed the girl at the deep-fried Oreo stand.

Just do me a favor, Emika's like. Look into his eyes and tell me you don't see what I see.

I look into his eyes and I see love. I see hate and anger. I see revolution and honor and dishonor all at once.

And I go, Okay, yeah, he seems like a cool guy.

He vomits into a bucket.

I'm scared, she's like. The white lady keeps talking about this new mega-president they're building. Bigger. Smarter. Better. When that new guy's ready, what's going to happen to Waj'm?

And I'm like, I'm sure there's a plan.

And she's like, Yeah, the plan is they're going to kill him.

You don't know that.

She starts shaking: I do know that. They're going to kill him. We need to do something, we can't just let them . . .

And seeing her all agitated like that is making the monster agitated, and he starts shaking and growling menacingly.

And I'm like, Emika, you need to calm down. I take a step toward her and Waj'm full-on freaks out, roaring and yanking on his chain, face all red.

TYRANNY AND OPPRESSION, ABIGAIL, he's like.

What the fuck? I'm like.

Emika goes, It's okay, Waj'm. Shh. It's okay. I'm safe; you're safe.

And Waj'm whimpers softly.

See, Emika says. He wants to protect me. That's what love is. And we need to protect him.

And I'm like, Why we? I got enough problems just trying to hold on to my job. Why do I have to be involved with this part of it?

And she's like, Because you have a good heart.

And I'm like, Yeah, I don't know about that. I definitely don't have the heart of ten men.

And she goes, No, but maybe two or three men.

And she smiles through her tears, and I think, How could I say no to that face?

You look really beautiful, I'm like.

I cringe as soon as I say it, because "You look really beautiful" is one of the things you're not supposed to say to your coworkers as outlined in the park staff behavioral guidelines, and also, just in general, that's a pretty dumb thing to say to a girl as she's telling you how much she loves another man—no, ten men in one man's body.

But Emika smiles at me, and she's like, Of course I do. I'm in love.

So I'm like, Well, let's see what happens, but just in the meantime, don't do anything crazy, right?

And she's like, Yeah, no, of course.

Mr. Gupta calls me into his office during my lunch break. White lady from the Frank and Felicity Fielding Foundation is there too, all smiles.

This is good news, he's like. We're very happy with the work you've been doing with Chester A. Arthur.

And I'm like, That is good news. Thank you!

And he's like, Yeah. But we're discontinuing the character.

What?! Why? How are people going to learn about the Pendleton Reform Act?!

And the white lady smiles and says, FieldingCorp is building a new hybrid president. We're about a week away from completion.

Mr. Gupta goes, When the new hybrid comes in, we're going to transition you to a new role. We were thinking . . . Jimmy Carter?

So now I'm thinking, Hot shit, I've hit the big time. But also, I did not realize that the new president-monster was going to be done so quickly. That is not great for the current president-monster, and any women who happen to be in love with him.

And Mr. Gupta's like, By the way, please don't tell anyone about the conversation we had in here. This information is obviously very delicate.

And I'm like, Oh, totally, yeah.

That night, I go to visit Ramona in the hospital, and I tell her the whole story.

I feel like Emika's about to do something rash, I'm like, but her heart is so pure and good.

And Ramona's like, Yeah, I don't know, this chick sounds crazy. I think you just got the hots for her.

And I'm like, Maybe . . . but what if she's right and Waj'm's in real danger?

And Ramona's like, Yeah, that's a good point, I didn't think about that. Okay, do what the hot chick says.

But on the other hand, Mr. Gupta's a good guy too, and it feels shitty to lie to him, especially since now he's giving me this promotion.

And Ramona goes, Yeah, this is what the guy at the deli counter calls a real pickle. Oh, I know what you should do!

What?

And she goes, Just think—who's your guy again?

And I go, Well, Chester A. Arthur for now, but next week they're moving me over to Jimmy Carter.

And she goes, Wow, okay. So just think—what would Chester A. Arthur and/or Jimmy Carter do?

How the fuck should I know? They never had to deal with this bullshit.

Okay, I'm going to go to sleep—I think they're going to do surgery on me again in the morning.

And I'm like, Again? Why?

And she's like, I don't know, I've lost track. Maybe last time one of the surgeons left her engagement ring inside me, so now she's hoping to get it back. Anyway, let me know how your thing all shakes out, okay?

I think about Ramona's advice. The truth is, if Chester A. Arthur ever found himself in this situation, I think he would probably suck up to the higher authority and tell Mr. Gupta that Emika's been having a secret affair with the mutant creature chained up in the white lady's office. Chester A. Arthur was always doing shit like that— I mean, not *exactly* like that, but similar.

On the other hand, Jimmy Carter seems like a softie and I feel like he would probably protect his friend's secret, so I guess if I'm going to be Jimmy Carter, I should probably do it the Jimmy Carter way.

Next day, I show up to work and the police are there.

What's going on? I'm like.

And Benjamin Harrison's like, Waj'm flew the coop.

And I'm like, No shit?

Harrison goes, Amir showed up this morning, and Miguel was

totally out of it. They think he got roofied. The whole thing's pretty hilarious.

Why's it hilarious? I'm like.

And he's all, 'Cause the park was working good before all these big-money tech people started playing God. Serves 'em right. You can't replace real people with artificial people.

And I'm all, Tell that to your extra-large fuck-doll.

And he goes, That's a completely different thing and you know it.

Everyone gets called in for meetings with Mr. Gupta and the white lady, one at a time.

Do you know anything? Mr. Gupta's like.

And I'm like, I never know anything about anything.

The white lady leans in, like, You understand that was company property, right? That hybrid is worth hundreds of thousands of dollars.

And I'm like, Really got your money's worth, huh?

And Mr. Gupta's like, All right, well, if you hear something, you'll let us know?

And I'm like, Yeah, of course.

I head out of Mr. Gupta's office and turn right into Wardrobe.

Emika's in there, smiling tightly, while the police go through her things.

Hey, can I talk to you for a minute? I'm like.

And Emika's like, Not right now, no.

Maybe like outside, for a minute, I could talk to you, I'm like.

And Emika's like, Really not a good time, but I'd love to talk later.

Just then my phone rings. It's Mom. I step outside and answer.

Where the hell are you? she's like.

I'm at work, Mom. I'm in the middle of—

Okay, well, I just wanted to call because your sister's going into surgery today and you don't even care.

I do care, Mom. I care a lot.

But she's not done talking. You don't care about your sister's cancer, she's like.

And I'm like, Don't say that. Don't say that word.

What word? "Cancer"? That's what she's got—you know that, right?

Yeah, Mom, I know, but Ramona's sickness is like the sun, okay? I can't look directly at it.

And she's like, Well, you need to look directly at it, because she could die—

And I go, She's not gonna die, Mom. The doctors know what they're doing.

She could die, Mom continues, and you're going to live the rest of your life knowing that you couldn't be there because you had to "work."

And I go, Why do you say "work" like that? "Work." It's not "work," it's *work,* okay? It's my job. I can't not go to work. Things are very precarious right now. I am dealing with situations that you can't even—

Your sister is going into surgery and she is very scared.

And I'm like, You want to get a job? 'Cause if not, who is going to pay for this surgery?

And she's like, You know I can't work on account of my shaky hands.

And I go, I know, Mom. Could you put Ramona on please?

I wander into the midway and linger by the McKinley Shooting Gallery.

Ramona takes the phone and goes, I wish you were here. Mom is being so crazy.

And I go, I wish I was there too. How are you doing? Mom says you're scared?

And Ramona goes, Naw, you know Mom likes to freak out. I'm gonna be fine.

And I'm like, That's what I told her!

And I hear Mom on the other side go, You think you're invincible, you don't understand how serious this is.

And I'm like, What, is she *trying* to scare you?

And Ramona laughs and is like, Yeah, Mom, why are you *trying* to scare me?

I make eye contact with Amir from Security across the midway and he starts heading over.

And I'm like, Look, I gotta go, but I love you, okay?

And Ramona goes, Yeah, yeah, I know.

I hang up the phone, and I'm like, Hey, Amir, crazy stuff, right? Wow.

And he's like, You were here pretty early yesterday.

And I go, Amir, I don't know what you're thinking—

And he cuts me off: Hey, man, the monster was there when I left work yesterday and gone when I showed up today. What happens on Miguel's shift is not my problem, and I'm not looking to stir shit for no reason.

And I'm like, I don't want to stir shit either, man. Like that's like my number one thing, is Don't stir shit.

And Amir's like, Uh-huh. I'm just saying, 'cause you've always been a good guy to me and I don't know what kind of crazy you're mixed up with now, but if they don't get any leads off of these interviews, they're going to crack open that security footage, and then they're going to know who's been going in what rooms.

And I'm like, Oh shit.

Yeah, so I'm just thinking if I'm you, maybe I'd want to get ahead of things and rat out the real troublemaker while the ratting out's good.

Word trickles down that the park's going to open as usual, while the police continue the investigation, so we should all get into wardrobe and to our starting locations. I plant myself near the Bridge to a Better Tomorrow, but I have trouble focusing.

I text Emika, "What the fuck is going on?"

And she texts back, "I swear I have no idea."

Cops are still roaming the grounds, but so as not to alarm the guests, Mr. Gupta's put them all in costumes. Wardrobe's got these extra suits, on account of the park always preps an alternate on election years in case the other guy wins. So now suddenly we've got guys like Dole and Dukakis and Romney silently drifting through the park like ghosts.

At one point, a family comes over to take their picture with me. Dad goes, very excited, We were told we should come talk to you about the Pendleton Reform Act.

I have no idea what he's talking about.

At lunch, I get a text message from my mom. It says: "Get here now."

I call her, but she doesn't pick up.

I call again, but she doesn't pick up.

I sneak out of the park, stashing my costume and giant Chester A. Arthur head behind some bushes near the entrance to the Trail of Tears Tram and snag the next bus to the hospital, where I meet a doctor outside Ramona's room.

I'm like, What's going on?

Doctor's like, Well, what we've got is a classic good news/bad news situation here. The surgery was a success, but now she's not waking up.

And I'm like, What do you mean she's not waking up? What are you saying, she's dead?

No, not dead, no! She's just comatose.

You put her in a coma?!

Yes, but we believe we've rooted out the source of her symptoms, so if she wakes up, she's all good!

And I'm like, *IF?!*

Then he says a whole bunch of big doctor words that I don't understand, and shows me some charts and x-rays, and ends the whole thing by going, As I said, the surgery was a success.

But she's in a coma, I'm like.

And he's like, Yes.

If my sister's in a coma, I'd say the surgery was not a fucking success, was it?

He's like, I can see you're very upset. We are monitoring your sister's condition and we will keep you informed of any—

Just then, his phone rings, and he's like, I'm sorry, I have to take this. My daughter's finding out what colleges she got into, it's a very exciting time. He answers his phone, like, Hello? Princeton?! That's incredible! and walks away.

I knock on the door and Mom slips into the hallway.

I'm like, What the hell are you thinking, not answering your phone?

And she's like, Where were you? You should have been here.

Oh, you think if I was here, the doctors would have said, Oh, let's *not* put her in a coma? You think I was the missing ingredient?

And she's like, You're right. I'm stupid. It's good that you never show up.

And I go, I'm sorry, Mom. Okay? You're right. I'm sorry. Did the doctors tell you anything else?

No. There's no news. No one will talk to me.

Well, you'll let me know if anything changes, right?

And she's like, Come into the room. Sit down.

I can't go in there, I'm like. I can't see her like that. When she wakes up, I'll come back.

And Mom's like, What if she doesn't wake up? What if she dies?

And I'm like, Well, if she dies then it doesn't make a difference if I see her now or if I see her when she's dead, right?

And Mom's like, What is wrong with you?

And I'm like, I gotta go back to work, Mom.

I try to sneak back into the park, but Mr. Gupta spots me.

Where the hell have you been? he's like.

And I'm like, I'm sorry—my sister—

And he's like, This is not a good day, you understand? Waj'm Maj'vht is still missing, so this is not the time to make it look like I can't keep track of my presidents.

And I go, Look, the thing about Waj'm is he's a ten-foot-tall stitched-up clone-mutant made of presidents. I feel like he's going to turn up. Maybe everyone doesn't need to be freaking out so much. This is not life or death.

It *is* life or death, Mr. Gupta's like. I'm going to get fired over this. I've put everything into this park. I have a family. You must understand that. If you know something—anything at all—please tell me.

And I'm like, Look, man, nobody tells me anything around here.

I'm barely back in position by the Bridge to a Better Tomorrow, when I see a man with an unfamiliar big giant head on the other side of the river, gesturing for me to come over.

I think it's Al Gore.

I gesture back like, *Who, me?*

And he gestures like, *Yeah, get over here.*

I hustle over to him and I'm thinking, Fuck, now I gotta answer a bunch of questions for the police and this is probably going to go on some sort of permanent criminal record and my mom is going to drop a heavy shit when she finds out and should I be calling a lawyer for this because I do not know any lawyers and this is definitely not what I signed up for when I applied to be a president.

But Al Gore doesn't say anything. Instead he indicates that I should follow him and he starts walking. He takes me to the Panama Canal, an indoor river ride that got boarded up five years ago on account of some of the animatronics turned out to be culturally insensitive.

We slip in a back entrance, and in the dark, nestled in shrubbery, I can make out the outline of a sleeping Waj'm Maj'vht, and I hear him muttering in his sleep: Duplicity . . . Yams . . .

I turn to Al Gore and I'm like, Listen, man, I don't know how this guy got in here, I've got nothing to do with this.

Al Gore takes off his big giant Al Gore head. It's Emika.

What the fuck? I'm like. Why did you text me and say you didn't know where he was?

Emika's like, You don't think they're tracking our phones?

Look, this is deep shit now, okay? Waj'm is very valuable property.

He's not property, okay? You can't own a person!

I explode, Most of Waj'm owned people!

She rolls her eyes and goes, That was like two hundred years ago.

And I go, There are security cameras all over this place. We are both gonna be in a hard fuck-load of trouble, like any minute now.

Emika shakes her head. Those things don't work; they're just there to scare you.

How do you know that?

Because I've been in the security office! The only monitors they got are connected to cameras at the entrances and exits to the park—which is why we haven't left the park yet.

It's not too late, I'm like. If you came clean to Mr. Gupta now—if he got to be the one to return Waj'm to the guys at FieldingCorp—

And Emika shouts, Waj'm is not going back to FieldingCorp!

And Waj'm rouses from his slumber and roars a mighty Waj'm roar.

And I'm like, Hey, shh, keep it the fuck down. How long do you think you can keep this guy a secret here?

And Emika's like, Well, I was hoping you could help me. You have a van, right?

And I'm like, No, I don't have a van.

And she's like, I thought you had a van.

And I'm like, No, man, I take the bus.

And she's like, Why did I think you had a van?

And I'm like, I don't understand why you think any of the things you think!

But then it hits me, and I immediately hate myself for saying out loud: Harrison has a van.

Emika's eyes go wide. Which Harrison?

Benjamin Harrison. It's where he keeps his fuck-doll.

And she's like, Oh my God, will you talk to him for me? I need that van.

Why don't you talk to him yourself?

I'm not friends with him like you are! Please, President Arthur? Will you talk to Benjamin Harrison for me?

It's never occurred to me before, but I think Emika doesn't even know my real name.

And I go, Yeah, I'll connect you to Harrison, but just from now on, leave me out of it, okay? I don't want to have anything to do with your plans, I don't want to know about them, I'm not involved, okay?

And she goes, Yeah, just help me get that van and I will never bother you with this again.

So I talk to Harrison, and at first he's like, Why should I help her out? That stuck-up bitch has always treated me like I'm a weirdo. And now she wants my fuck-doll wagon? Well, who's the weirdo now?

And I'm like, Just think of it like you're in an X-Men movie. And Waj'm is the mutant who's being persecuted, and you're the X-Men, and he needs you to save him.

And Harrison considers this and then goes, Okay, but after we put him in my van, what's the next part of the plan?

And I'm like, I don't know, talk to Emika. I don't want to have anything to do with it.

And he's like, Is she going to need me to bring my swords?

I go back to my post and just try to be Chester A. Arthur for a little bit. I think about how, no matter which way this all breaks, this is probably one of the last times I'm ever going to be Chester A. Arthur, and honestly it feels kind of bittersweet. I think about how shitty the real President Arthur must have felt at the convention when—after the Pendleton Reform Act—his own party wouldn't even nominate him for reelection. I feel kind of bad for abandoning President Arthur, just like everybody else, but also I feel more and more like, in the world of politics, you've got to look out for yourself, because it's not like anyone else is going to be looking out for you.

Suddenly, there's a large crash from the other side of the park and the screeching of van wheels. Possibly gunfire? A crowd runs past me, but I stay planted at the Bridge to a Better Tomorrow, because of like I said earlier, looking out for myself and all.

I get a call from Emika and I ignore it.

I get a call from Harrison and I ignore it.

After all, you're not supposed to use your phone in costume. Park policy.

A few minutes later, Buchanan ambles by and says, Hey, man, Mr. Gupta wants to see you in his office. White lady too.

I start to head over, but then I think: This is stupid.

So I leave.

I take a bus to the hospital and I turn my phone off.

I leave my phone off for days and I sit with Ramona while she sleeps.

I talk to her and sing her songs, and when I'm not talking to her I'm talking to Mom. I'm telling Mom that everything's going to be okay, that Ramona loves her and wouldn't leave her, that Ramona's strong. And finally, I understand why my mother wanted me here.

At some point I drift off, and I'm awakened by gentle shouting: Hey! Wake up, dummy!

It's Ramona, smiling weakly.

And she's like, What, are you gonna sleep the whole day away? Let's get this show on the road.

How long have you been awake?

And she goes, I dunno. A few minutes?

I look around. Where's Mom?

And Ramona's like, I don't know, man. I just woke up. Now I gotta be the one to keep track of everybody?

I press the button on the side of her bed that calls the doctor.

And she's like, Hey, whatever happened with all that shit that was going on with your job?

And I'm like, Yeah, I don't think it's going to work out.

She goes, You liked that job.

And I go, Naw, I didn't like it that much.

And she goes, But what happened with the girl you liked? And the monster? And the new monster that they were gonna bring in?

And I go, I don't know. I'm telling you, man, I've been here.

And she goes, Were you here the whole time I was asleep? You didn't have to do that.

I didn't, I say. I wasn't. I got here too late. Mom was here, though. The whole time.

Ramona smiles and goes, Yeah, Mom's crazy like that.

And I go, Yeah.

And I think about how loving someone is kind of like being president, in that it doesn't change you, not really. But it brings out more of the you that you already are.

We will be close
on Friday 18 July.
Sorry for any
inconvinience

We will be close on Friday 18 July.

We will be so close on Friday 18 July. For one night only I will hold your face in my hands and I will kiss you quickly and then slowly and then quickly, and we will feel this incredible connection, and we will tell each other *everything*.

On Friday 18 July, we will feed each other berries, and we will sing-mumble-slur old half-remembered camp songs, and we will laugh about how there was a time, not even that long ago, when we hadn't even met, and what were we *doing* not meeting, who were we fooling, whose time were we wasting?

Sitting on my bed, recalling the origin of your knee's crescent-moon scar, you'll gesticulate wildly and I'll watch the cigarette sparks dance like evaporating fireflies, dizzy for a home in our trail of discarded clothing.

"I want to know you completely," I'll whisper into every crevice of your body, as if such a thing were ever possible. We'll make up constellations out of the freckles on our thighs, rich mythologies of long-dead ancient civilizations.

"Did you know I can juggle?" you'll say, and I'll say, "Show me."

Every other night will have been rehearsal for Friday 18 July—we had to be ready. Everything was pushing us imperceptibly toward this moment—if I hadn't missed that train, if you hadn't moved for the job, just *imagine*.

"I don't want it to be tomorrow," you'll sigh, a single tear escaping as you laugh bitterly at the futility of the sentiment. "I want it to be Friday 18 July forever."

And when the morning comes, our love like bugs will scatter in the light. We will dress ourselves while facing the wall, we will scramble for our phones, we will be strangers.

And we will realize that Friday 18 July, like every day in history before it, was a moment, a twenty-four-hour trick of the light, a thing that happened once and never again.

And that sad truth will just about swallow us whole.

Sorry for any inconvinience

Acknowledgments

Before I wrote a book, I always pictured the act of writing a book to be a very solitary pursuit, especially compared to the boisterous world of TV writing, the collaborative art of playwriting, and the high-flying derring-do of skywriting. This may still be true for most books—I've only written just the one—but this particular book would not be possible without the helpful participation of many smart and kind people who are not me, and I am very grateful for them.

First of all, I'd like to thank Tim O'Connell and Anna Kaufman at Knopf. I k'not have asked for a better team to cheer me on, bounce ideas across, and gently guide me away from my worst impulses with the occasional well-deployed "Are we sure about this one?"

I'd also like to thank our production editor, Rita Madrigal; copyeditor, Nancy Tan; and proofreaders, Tricia Wygal and Lawrence Krauser. The editing process has been a wonderful journey of discovery about how little I still understand about where hyphens belong. (The general theme of these acknowledgments is: Thank you for helping me look less stupid.)

As of writing this note, it is unclear how much I should thank publicists Nimra Chohan and Madison Brock and marketers Julianne Clancy and Emily Wilkerson because the seeds of their labor have yet to blossom, but if you are reading this book now then they did their job well, and I am thankful to them!

Also, this book is so pretty! I have our jacket designer, Tyler Comrie, and text designer, Cassandra Pappas, to thank for that!

Acknowledgments

Many people have read these stories over the years and given me their feedback. I'd like to particularly acknowledge Caroline Damon, Dan Moyer, Stephanie Staab, Shary Niv, Jessica Hempstead, Lindsay Meisel, Suzanne Richardson, Natasha Vargas-Cooper, Julie Buntin, Lorraine DeGraffenreidt, Octavia Bray, Karen Joseph Adcock, Becky Bob-Waksberg, and Amalia Bob-Waksberg. I'm sure there are many wonderful people I'm forgetting here, as well as many terrible people I am omitting on purpose, so if you don't see your name here, rest assured you are in one of those two groups.

I'd like to be very Hollywood for a moment and thank my reps, particularly Mollie Glick and Rachel Rusch at CAA and Joel Zadak at Artists First, for helping these stories find a home.

In the spring of 2017, some of these pieces were read out loud at the Upright Citizens Brigade Theatre in Los Angeles. If you're ever putting together a book of short stories, I highly recommend you put on a show to see what's working; it's tremendously helpful. That show was produced by Lorraine DeGraffenreidt, and the stories were read by the very talented Natalie Morales, Baron Vaughn, Will Brill, Emma Galvin, and Kate Berlant. Thank you to everyone who helped me put that show together and everyone who attended it.

I am greatly indebted to some wonderful teachers who encouraged me to write in high school and college, specifically Jim Shelby, Paul Dunlap, Rachel Lurie, Chiori Miyagawa, and Dominic Taylor, among others.

I'd like to thank my family, immediate, extended, and metaphorical, for years of love and support.

Finally, I would like to thank my wife. About half of these stories are from before I met her and half since, and I'm convinced if you lined them all up in the order they were written, you could pinpoint the moment where my heart became whole.

"We Men of Science" originally published in *WHAT YOU DO | EAT A PEACH* in 2009 and subsequently in *Catapult* on September 10, 2015. "Missed Connection—m4w" originally published in the Missed Connections section of Craigslist.com on August 6, 2013.

Raphael Bob-Waksberg is the creator and executive producer of the Netflix series *BoJack Horseman*. This is his first book.

A NOTE ON THE TYPE

This book was set in Caledonia, a Linotype face designed by W. A. Dwiggins (1880–1956). It belongs to the family of printing types called "modern face" by printers—a term used to mark the change in style of the type letters that occurred around 1800. Caledonia borders on the general design of Scotch Roman but it is more freely drawn than that letter.

Composed by North Market Street Graphics,
Lancaster, Pennsylvania

Printed and bound by Berryville Graphics,
Berryville, Virginia

Designed by Cassandra J. Pappas